DOG WALK DI

A Ron Webb

Pete Jennings

Gruff Books © 2021

12, Carlton Close, Gt. Yeldham

Halstead, Essex U.K. CO9 4QJ

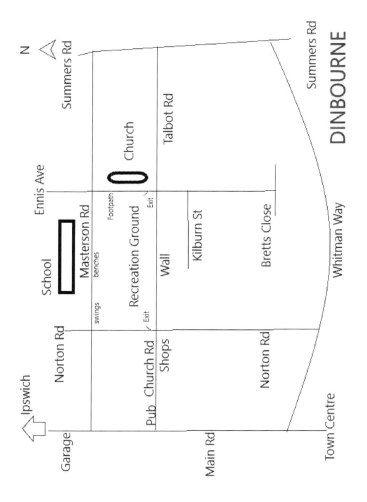

made much more of a grunt. Unsure whether the blow had been fatal, the villain struck twice more to finish the job. The head became a hideous mess of blood, hair, skin and bone, and the attacker tried to avoid looking at what they had done. Then breathing raggedly, they dropped the pipe and grabbed the shoulders of the victim, the jacket cloth tearing at their fingernails with the strain. The assassin dragged him face downwards along the rough ground to behind the bush where they had been waiting. It required a lot of effort even for this lightly built body, and they were still breathing heavily as they bent down to check the pockets: a mobile phone and a wallet were extracted with difficulty from the jeans. Everybody nowadays watched enough tv shows to know that it was best to remove the identity if you could.

In the desperation to escape unseen, the slayer forgot to retrieve the now blood-splattered pipe on the ground and had to walk back a dozen paces to it, cursing. Squatting down to retrieve it, they looked around. There were no cars or pedestrians to be seen, and they strode swiftly off in the same direction as the young man had been heading. Reaching the Talbot Road gate opposite the church, the murderer turned right onto the footpath, then quickly right again to where their car was parked at Kilburn Street entrance. No houses overlooked it, and they shakily pressed the keyfob to unlock the vehicle.

Inside, the gory pipe was dumped on the passenger side floor. They needed to thoroughly wipe the blood and prints off it before putting it back where it belonged, hidden in plain sight. There had been no chance to obtain rubber gloves beforehand. The wallet was opened, and fifty pounds in notes and a couple of pound coins were found. Stuffing the money into their pockets, they left the wallet on the passenger seat with the phone. Pausing, they then thought it would be advisable to wipe them for fingerprints. Looking around, a spray can of de-icer was found to douse them liberally. They thoroughly wiped each item with tissues from the glove compartment and dropped them on the floor with the pipe.

The killer decided to ditch them on the way home. The sooner, the better. They knew that it would be incriminating if the phone or bank card left inside the wallet were used or found on them. Finally, the individual shakily turned the ignition and headed away on Talbot Road, pausing only to dump the items in a hedge a mile away from the scene of the crime. They should not be connected with the body there.

The driver was conscious of keeping to the speed limit, not a thing they were usually overly cautious about. The last thing they wanted was to be stopped by the police. Reaching home, the car was carefully parked, and they tried to get control of their nerves. 'Think!' Looking down at themself using the motor's interior light, they could see some blood spots on their navy tracksuit top. It was pulled off, and the pipe and discarded tissues wrapped in it. Ensuring that no neighbours were on their doorsteps, the murderer walked around the side of the house to the back garden and slid the package underneath the raised shed's floor. They could be dealt with that later, and the pipe returned to where it belonged. The hut was locked, and the key was indoors. Right now, a stiff drink inside was needed.

As the criminal drank a second large shot of cheap whisky, the reality of what they had done became clear. This evening was a much higher level of crime than what they had become involved in before. Yet one thing had led to another, and that onto more. It seemed that they had no choice. So long as they continued to act naturally tomorrow, there was no reason for them to be a suspect, was there?

Jim had reached Veronica. He seemed to be turning her away from the bushes and holding onto her dogs as well as his own.

Gilly had already left the field by the Talbot Road exit with her charges, oblivious of what was going on behind her. As the other dog walkers got nearer, Jim put his hand up. "I shouldn't come any nearer", he commanded. "There is a chap down there with his head bashed in – blood everywhere", he explained. Stan handed the lead of James to his wife, Louise. "I'm a trained First Aider", he commented, explaining to the others and moving forward around the bush where a pair of feet could be seen.

Veronica was suddenly sick on the ground, and Jim moved the dogs away from her and the pool of vomit. Sandra stepped forward and, Veronica burst into tears. "It's … it's horrible", she muttered in between sobs. Stan emerged from the bush, looking white-faced, shocked and sad. "No pulse – he has been there for a while, I reckon," he said quietly.

"I will dial the Emergency services," said Louise, reaching in her pocket for a mobile phone. "Police and Ambulance, I think." The others could hear her conversation: "Police and Ambulance. The Recreation Ground between Church Road and Talbot Road. There is a man on the ground with serious head injuries, believed dead. No, I don't know his name. My name is Louise Bennett. We were walking our dog. Yes, I will stay here – 07778 693465. Thank you." She pocketed the phone. "They will be here soon", she announced self-importantly and probably needlessly.

"It's a wonder that Gilly didn't notice him", commented John. "She went along here first this morning. Mind you, she was probably on her phone." The others nodded quietly, each with their thoughts. Only the victim's feet could be seen protruding from beyond the bush, but Rex sniffed out some blood on the ground, just a couple of yards further up the track. Jim pulled him away but proudly praised him as a good dog for finding it.

"No doubt the Police will want to ask us all some daft fool questions when they arrive, so I think we'd better all stay", announced John authoritatively. "Mind you don't tramp around the area, though: they'll want to see if there are any footprints or other clues." Then he walked a little way away from the group to get a better angle to view the body and pull out his mobile phone.

"Suffolk Argus? Put me straight through to Billy Mills – this is John Westrup here. You know, your old Sub Editor. It's urgent – a news scoop for you!" A hurried conversation ensued, and John promised to stay until a reporter arrived. "If you get here fast, you may get a picture as well before they seal the area off", he added, "in time for the weekly edition on Friday." (The company published several local titles, most of which were weeklies.)

However, a local police patrol car arrived, followed in quick succession by several others. "Crime Scene – Do not enter" tape was rapidly strung across the two gateways. A Sergeant took control and detailed Constables to put a barrier around the bush area, move the public and their dogs back, look for evidence on the ground and not disturb what was to him a crime scene. One unfortunate young Constable who had earlier annoyed the Sergeant by straying too near was given the unenviable job of checking the litter bins and dog waste bins at the two entrances and the fenced-off playground. This action was much to the amusement and relief of his colleagues.

Another serious-looking Constable slowly took down brief statements from everybody in turn. A couple of white-suited Scene of Crime Officers (SOCO) took photographs and erected a plastic tent over the body. An ambulance arrived at the gate, but having spoken to the Constable on duty, the crew stayed aboard, waiting to remove the body. John spotted a furiously waving figure near the ambulance and went over to talk to the eager but frustrated newspaper reporter through the wire netting fence that formed a barrier to Norton Road.

"They will not let you anywhere near now," he said, "but your photographer may be able to get a long lens shot of the tent from around the corner on Masterson Road. We don't know who he is, and he is face-down anyway. I would guess that from his clothes, he is about 20-30 years old. I reckon CID will be here from Ipswich soon. There is a lot of blood: he probably got hit from behind." After asking after a couple of his former colleagues' health, John sauntered back towards his morning companions with Fi.

Veronica was now hunched, sniffling into a tissue provided by an understanding Sandra. "Would you like me to walk home with you when we are allowed to go?" she asked, not sure of how else she could try to help.

"Thanks for the offer, but no thanks", responded Veronica. "I am over the worst now, but it was such a horrible shock. It will be a job to get that scene out of my mind. I'll have a cup of sweet tea and go to bed when I get home. I work the night shift at the bakery," she added in explanation. Sandra looked down at the spaniels. "Well, Pat and Billy, you make sure you give your mum lots of cuddles and licks today", she instructed with a smile.

"Now that they've had their walk, they will be getting my feet warm again at the bottom of my bed," said Veronica, trying to put on a brave smile.

Although she hadn't seen the body, Sandra felt quite shaken herself and later put extra sugar in her tea as well as raiding the biscuit tin when she got home. As a treat, she broke a piece off for Jimbo. He was looking up at her expectantly, head tilted adoringly to one side with the uncanny knack and steady gaze of a born scrounger. When all sign of any more treats faded, he attacked his toy rat with enthusiasm, shaking it from side to side and making Sandra giggle.

Chapter 3. Tuesday 6th October. Ipswich.

The Police Sergeant at Dinbourne had contacted Ipswich CID as soon as he had verified the situation on-site. Detective Chief Inspector Ron Webb smoothly steered his Rover car through Ipswich's morning traffic to get onto the A-road that would take him and Detective Sergeant Colin Newton to Dinbourne. Ron was a bit of an old-timer, sometimes deficient in coping with new politically correct times, but with a good arrest record and the image of solid dependability that re-assured his bosses that he was a 'safe pair of hands.' His neat haircut, dark blue suit, white shirt, polished black shoes and conservative tie had failed to influence his younger assistant's fashion choices: black leather bomber jacket over a pastel yellow shirt, red tie and grey needlecord trousers. For Ron, though, it was the tousled 'just out of bed' hairstyle that bothered him most, although he was too much of a gent to comment.

The other annoying characteristic of his passenger was a propensity to chatter on car journeys, and he was doing it now. Something about an international rugby match last night, but Ron wasn't concentrating as the car shook in the wake of a container lorry passing them at speed on the dual carriageway. They were just passing the enormous British Telecom Research Laboratories, which dominated the local skyline.

A prominent tower was topped with a block that was twisted 45 degrees from the alignment with its base. The seventies built concrete blocks gave way to an industrial estate on the left and housing on the right as they negotiated a few roundabouts before hitting open countryside.

As they drove under a flyover and round a larger roundabout, a kestrel hovered seeking breakfast, but Ron lost sight of it as they joined the Ipswich bypass. Colin's stream of chatter was interrupted by a call from base asking for an estimated arrival time to the crime scene, which he answered.

By now, they were heading over the Orwell Bridge that spanned the river in a graceful arc. Unfortunately, the protective walls precluded seeing the vista of shoreline and water heading towards the estuary between Felixstowe and Harwich. Colin Newton prattled on:

"Another body found by a dog walker. I reckon they're all a bit suspicious, the number of times they crop up. Maybe we should keep tags on them? Who the heck would want to go out in the early morning in wind and rain, picking up poo and paying vets bills for something that spoils the furniture and needs babysitting? It beats me."

"No appreciation for someone that always enjoys when you are talking to it?" jibed Newton. The sarcasm went over Colin's head, and he carried on regardless:

"I prefer curtain twitchers as witnesses. They usually know everybody and are usually full of useful little details."

"You may have a point there, Colin", growled Ron as he took the slip road and turned off the roundabout to the A14 dual carriageway towards Bury St. Edmunds. The traffic was thinning, and he was able to go at a steady 70 mph.

Further information about the incident came over the police radio, answered by Colin. "Subject is a deceased male. Uniform have cordoned off the crime scene, and Scene of Crime Officers are already there. Nobody witnessed the death, but the witnesses finding the body are detained at the scene. The ambulance service is standing by. Over"

"What do you reckon then, sir?" asked Colin after acknowledging the radio message. "Fight? Mugging? Drugs?"

"Based on long years of experience, I reckon it is whatever we find when we get there", replied Webb sourly. Newton finally had the sense to shut up until they arrived.

About twelve miles out from Ipswich, they turned off the A14 onto the road into Dinbourne. As they passed a petrol station on the Main Road, they came into housing estate added to Dinbourne after the war in the 1950s. The Main Road eventually led to a much older town square, with some 16th century timbered houses dating back to its history as one of Suffolk's prosperous wool towns. The wealth had also created an imposing ancient church, and there were also rows of pleasant Georgian pink fronted houses with the decorative plasterwork known in Suffolk as pargetting.

Webb knew roughly where the Recreation Ground was situated and soon found it by turning left onto Church Rd before the road continued towards the town centre. They passed a pub and shops and tried to find a place to park amongst the line of uniform's squad cars, ambulance, SOCO van and some interested bystanders. Getting out of the motor, Webb headed quickly to the field, resolutely ignoring the shouted questions of a newspaper reporter and leaving Colin to follow in his wake. He flashed his warrant card to the PC freezing on duty at the gate, whom he invariably thought looked too young to have left school.

A sergeant came towards him. "Hello, Sir! We have a male with his head bashed in. SOCO are in there taking pictures, and I have kept my chaps away from sticking their footprints down in the area, but it is hard and dryish. They have taken statements from all the dog walkers. They have also been fanning out, but no sign of a weapon yet. One of the dogs found some blood on the ground over there, so we have pegged it. There are also signs that he has been dragged from over there on the path and hidden behind the bush. There are a couple of scrapes in the soil where the feet possibly dragged along." He pointed, and the detectives peered down at the rust coloured patch and two scrape marks.

"Well done, Sergeant Bristow! It seems like you have done an excellent job here, thank you. Maybe you could organise someone to go round to the houses on the other side of the wall, in case they heard anything?"

"Certainly! Can the witnesses here be let go?" asked the Sergeant. "We have got all their details and statements."

"Which one found the body?" asked Ron. The Sergeant pointed. "Veronica Hedley", he added.

"OK, you can let the rest go, but I will just have a quick word with her." They introduced themselves to Veronica.

"Hello, I'm DCI Webb, and this is my colleague DS Newton. I understand that you found the body?"

"Yes, well, it was my two dogs really – Pat and Billy", she responded nervously. Ron made a great show of bending down and coaxing the pair of spaniels. "Good boy, good girl!" he said gently. "So you have been helping the police? Good dogs!" he added, smiling, which had the desired effect of calming Veronica. DS Newton kept well back, avoiding the dogs and getting his notebook out. "About what time was it that you reached here?" Ron asked.

" I got onto the field just before nine. I came in via the Talbot Road entrance over there," she said, pointing to a gateway in the direction of a modern church. "I initially went over to the other side and spoke to some of the other dog walkers. It was probably about twenty past nine by the time I walked around the field and reached here," continued Veronica. "Then I called out, and the others came over, but we tried not to disturb anything. Although Stan did go and check for a pulse – he used to work at the hospital. Then Louise rang for the Police and Ambulance."

"Was anybody else on the Recreation Ground when you arrived that we haven't spoken to?" chipped in Newton, still keeping his distance from the pair of spaniels that looked far too over-friendly to him. He didn't fancy muddy paw prints on his trousers.

"Only Gilly", replied Veronica. "She was here earlier as usual and was walking around the perimeter ahead of me. She must have passed the spot without noticing. She was on her phone, I think, and she had four dogs on leads."

"Four dogs must be quite a handful", commented Newton. "Do you know where we can get hold of her or what her surname is, please?"

"Oh no, I don't know her by anything else other than Gilly. The dogs aren't her's – she is a paid dog walker. I think she advertises as 'Walkies!' in the local paper – I have seen it."

"That is very helpful," said Ron. We can soon find her from that. Do any of you come over here in the evening?"

"No, it's too dark for me at this time of year, and I work a night shift. I doubt Gilly would do because she told me once that she works on the other side of town for the rest of the day. Stan and Louise only walk once per day but have talked about increasing it when the weather improves. I don't know about the other men: they have got bigger dogs, so they might go out a second time. Sandra (the lady who was with me just now) only walks her dog once per day. The lady with the cockapoo fits her dog walking with going backwards and forwards to the school with her children. I know the dog's name is Bella, but I am sorry that I don't remember hers. It is often the way."

"That's alright, you have been very helpful. You'd better go off and get yourself warm with a cup of tea now. Thank you once again," added Ron.

As Veronica hurried away with her dogs, one of the pair of Crime Scene Officers (CSO) forensic team emerged from the white tent, camera in hand. He was wearing a hooded all in one white plastic suit that rustled as he moved, plus gloves and overshoes. The detectives naturally gravitated towards him. "Have you got all you want?" queried Webb.

"Not quite", he answered. "The body is face down, so we thought we'd better wait until you'd seen it before we rolled it over. The Senior CSO pathologist is still inside the tent." He offered them white plastic overshoes and gloves from his kit, which they donned before following him in. "Good morning Dr Wilson" greeted Webb.

She straightened up from inspecting the crumpled corpse and turned. "Hello, Ron, and Colin, isn't it?" she replied. Deborah Wilson was in her thirties, and even with a plastic suit on, her shapely attractiveness was not lost on DS Newton, who beamed at having his name remembered by her. The back of the skull of the corpse was a mass of dried blood and hair. There were three depressed lines, and a shard of white bone could be seen protruding through the primary wound.

Without any preamble, Dr Wilson gave her brief verbal synopses of what she had seen so far:

at this time of year. There may be the odd jogger going around it during the day, but most of them stick to pavements."

"Wouldn't want their posh trainers to get mucky, I expect", commented Webb, a little disdainful of anyone who attempted exercise of any description.

"No muggings in Dinbourne either, since we put Waller away a year ago", added the Sergeant.

"Ah yes, I remember it", responded Newton. "You rendered a great service to the community", he added wryly. "Ah well, we'll be on our way then. Thanks very much, gentlemen," said DCI Webb, turning to go. "Keep a lookout for any missing person cases, though – that poor sod must have known someone."

On the way back to the car, Webb asked Newton to phone ahead to the murder squad in Ipswich and get them ready for a meeting as soon as he returned. As they drove back, Newton suddenly blurted out, "It couldn't have been a random mugging: nobody was going to wait there for someone to walk past at that time of night!"

"Yes, well done! You are thinking the right way," praised Ron. "We'll make a detective of you yet! I was thinking the very same thing." They drove back to Suffolk Police HQ at Martlesham, the other side of Ipswich.

Chapter 3. The afternoon of Tuesday 6th October, Dinbourne.

Sandra still felt shocked about what had happened this morning. The one positive part of her daily routine had been shattered. She was even unsure whether she wanted to go back there to walk Jimbo tomorrow morning. He wasn't too sure what was going on but sensed his owner was unhappy, so he jumped up on the armchair beside her and licked her ear. "Oh, bless you, Jimbo," she said and stroked his head. He was quite an independent little chap, but it felt right for him to be close beside her.

Gilly had a surprising telephone call from a policeman when he finally got past the engaged tone. She took it to be some sort of sick joke at first. Once convinced that he was genuine, she admitted that she had been oblivious to anybody in the bushes this morning and was quite shocked. Suppose it had been the attacker and not the victim? She felt pretty disconcerted that she had been close to something so grotesque (excluding her ex-husband.)

Norma was guiltily elated. She would finally have some genuine exclusive gossip to offer when she picked up the kids from school later this afternoon. As it happened, she was to be disappointed: every other parent was keen to get their children safely home in a hurry from whatever imagined terror stalked the area.

Meanwhile, John Westrup was trying to calm his wife down. Her mental state did not cope well with change. She was distraught that he arrived home late and since he told her why she was now is frightened that she would be murdered in her bed if he left the house again.

Louise Bennett would not stop criticising her husband for his actions on the field. Why didn't he check for breathing as well as the pulse? Why didn't Stan turn the chap over to see who it was? He also has blood smeared on the sleeve of his jacket where he got too near the corpse, and she is refused to put it in the wash with the other clothes – he must hand wash it himself. The result of all this is that Stan (who avoided arguing with her as a pointless activity) took himself off to his shed and pretended to be making stuff whilst swigging from a concealed half bottle of whisky and eating some forbidden chocolate that he hid there.

Veronica had a very different time. After failing to get off to sleep, she listlessly watched TV until her partner Linda came in and told her it was too loud and she could not work from home on the phone or concentrate on the computer with the noise. Linda was then taken aback when the usually solid Veronica burst into tears and described what she went through this morning. Linda then became very apologetic and guiltily made them some food of which Veronica ate hardly a mouthful. Despite pleas from Linda, she got ready and still went to work as usual at 6 pm.

It was about 2 pm when DCI Webb and DS Newton walked into their squad room, the other four team members looked up expectedly. Detective Constable Chris Winter, the newest member, had already set up a whiteboard with a blown-up map of the murder area and headings such as Name? Time of death? Known associates? Suspects?

Ron set to briefing them on what they had found out so far, which hardly filled in many of the spaces. He offered a few theories, as well: "It may be a mugging since no wallet was found. The attacker was likely to be a tall male since the first blow had to be struck from a height with some force. The attacker might have followed the victim from behind since it would be an unlikely place to lay in wait to make a random ambush unless this was a planned attack. I think that the victim will turn out to be local to the area because a stranger would not be so aware of a short cut between the two residential areas. We don't even know which direction he was travelling. Any other ideas, anybody?" With a general shaking of heads, it was a case of sharing out tasks:

"DC Christopher Winter to obtain any CCTV footage from the area and go through it, with help from anyone else available. DC Peggy

Catchpole to chase up missing person's reports from Dinbourne and the surrounding areas. DC Will Catesby organise printing out of the relevant photos when they arrive and get a police artist to draw the face since we cannot directly use a dead man's image if it's needed to circulate. You'd better cast the net wider once we get a useable picture." He instructed DS Newton to keep himself available to accompany him on any leads. "All of you know that the first 24 hours are crucial", he added. "We need the victim's name, address, job, friends, enemies, what he was doing there, and we need them damn fast. At the moment, we have nothing, so get to it! I'm off upstairs to put 'His Lordship' in the picture."

'His Lordship' was his nickname for his superior, Detective Superintendent Hardy, who spoke with a decidedly aristocratic tone compared to his junior officer's Suffolk accents. Webb privately thought of Hardy as an over-promoted college boy who said all the right things and was a skilled politician. He dealt with him on sufferance and necessity, but that didn't mean that he had to like or respect him. Webb had long dropped further promotion ideas since it meant dealing with even more officers like Hardy and not having the joy of catching criminals. His subtle way of rebelling against him was never to mention him by name unless he had to. Maybe then nobody would remember him.

Chris Winter, dressed in a new blue suit that he had treated himself to when he recently got his transfer to CID, had been jotting down the tasks against the officer's names on the board and then got onto a database listing known CCTV cameras. He was pleased to find that there was a single CCTV camera at a parade of shops near the Recreation Ground, but by the time he could reach it, they would be closed for the night, so he resolved to go there first thing in the morning and told DCI Webb as soon as he returned from his meeting. "Well done, son, that's the first bit of good news on this case", he commented. His Lordship wants something to tell the press, and I'm buggered if I know. I'll be in my office reviewing the statements and trying to come up with something."

The other officers had all scurried off and were glad to have something specific to do. Unfortunately, none of them produced any tangible results, and most of them went home late.

Chapter 3. Wednesday 7th October, Dinbourne.

Colin Newton rose early and showered to clear his head. It hadn't been a particularly late night, but he had not slept well, tossing and turning with the case on his mind and trying to think if there was another clue they were missing or an avenue unexplored. He had a sizeable unsweetened cup of black coffee with his muesli; he was trying to shed a bit of weight and went to the gym as regularly as his policing duties would allow. Colin took the stairs rather than the lift from his Waterside converted warehouse flat and walked along the old dock past the modern marina to his Volkswagen Polo car. The distinctive jingling of halyards rattling against yacht masts mixed with the cries of swooping gulls.

He reflected that he did not have enough money to play with each month between that car, gym membership, and the mortgage. He had bought the flat after his divorce from Helen. She was a solicitor he had met whilst still in uniform and not a person to be trifled with when she found out about his affair with Diane from the gym. He could ruefully recommend her firm for getting maximum financial settlements for their clients and had not been left with much as a deposit to put down on this place.

He drove the short distance to the Suffolk Police HQ at Martlesham, where the office was situated, arriving simultaneously with DCI Webb.

"Can you fix us some tea, please, then we can go through and see what the pathologist has got" rumbled Webb, never a morning person. He was sucking the first of many humbugs of the day, a habit he acquired after giving up smoking. Tea duly sipped, and the information about the CCTV was passed on. "It may at least show whether he walked from the shop's direction", commented Newton. "If we were fortunate, we may even see someone following him!"

" No, it's never like the TV cops – I'm not that lucky", retorted Webb pessimistically as they descended to the lab by lift. "Nobody leaves a cufflink or earing conveniently at the scene of the murder anymore either."

In contrast, Dr Deborah Wilson, in a fresh white coat and hair tied back in a ponytail and a whiff of perfume, was at her best in the morning and greeted the pair with a sunny smile. "Is it my scintillating company you have come to enjoy, or is it something more mundane like a dead body?" she asked rhetorically.

"Any progress on the body from the Dinbourne case, please Dr Wilson?" intoned Webb, almost formally and ignoring the cue to be pleasant.

"I'm afraid there is not much more information to add to what I said yesterday", she replied. "From his teeth, I would put him at about 20 years old. He had eaten a cheese sandwich earlier in the day, and there was a little alcohol in his system. Not enough to make him drunk, though. A bit on the skinny side, but not emaciated at 120 pounds, and he is only 5 foot 6 inches. I noticed he did chew his nails, so that he may have been anxious or depressed recently. There were no drugs present in his system and no other wounds other than the ones on his head. As I thought initially, the uppermost blow killed him with an internal haemorrhage and bone splinters penetrating the brain. It would have been relatively instant. The other two impacts are from a different angle, probably when he was already face down on the ground. It may have been something like a crowbar, but no wider than a quarter of an inch. I haven't found any fragments of the weapon in the wound, which indicates it was unlikely to be made of wood. As my colleague reported, he seems to have been dragged after death by the arms, face down. Some stitching had freshly burst around the sleeves of his teeshirt. We haven't found any foreign fibres or hairs on his clothes."

"Thank you very much, Dr Wilson," said Webb. "Any refinement on time?"

"He wasn't wearing a watch, so no smashed dial to inform us. Mobile phones showing the time must be the curse of jewellers and pathologists everywhere nowadays: nobody needs a watch anymore. From the temperatures and observations I took at the scene, compared to a second set I took here, I would estimate the death as between 7:30-8:30 pm, but it could be plus or minus an hour on either side. He was certainly killed before the frost came later that night, but being in a sheltered position skews it a bit. I am still typing it all up and will email it through to you later today if that's OK?"

"Perfect, thank you very much. That is very useful. I'm afraid that we haven't got a name to put to him yet for your forms, but we will let you know if we find out," concluded Webb. "Come on, Newton, we had better let this lady get on with her work." Reluctantly DS Colin Newton followed him out of the room, taking one glance back as he did. She was already engrossed with bending over the desk and looking at something down a microscope.

As they took the lift back to the office, Colin offered, "It looks like drugs are probably off the table, sir."

"Yes, and a meal too. Most people would have eaten a bit more than a cheese sandwich since breakfast time by 8 pm or whatever."

"Deborah did say that he had a little alcohol in his bloodstream. I'll go and check out the pub nearby – we passed it yesterday. The Cross Keys, I think it was."

"Good idea – catch them as they open. And it's Dr Wilson to you, DS Newton, please unless she says otherwise. She is a professional from another department!" DCI Webb expected certain old fashioned standards from his team.

"Yes sir, sorry sir", replied Newton sheepishly. He felt at times that his boss was curmudgeonly and old fashioned. He would also admit that he was a good mentor and gave him opportunities to shine and praise when he succeeded, so at least he was fair. He was saved from further embarrassment by DC Catesby in shirtsleeves and tie, waving a sheaf of paper at them. "Artists version of the face, plus details of the clothing, sir. I just got them."

"Thank you, DC Catesby," said Webb. "Can you make sure all the team get at least one each, and one goes up at the top of the whiteboard, please? Thanks." He studied his copy as he wandered over to DC Peggy Catchpole, the only female in his team. She was wearing a professional woman's grey trouser suit and blouse, which he privately thought very appropriate. He thought female officers who flashed their legs too much could be a distraction, which was rather unfair, but he was born to an older generation. He knew from her personnel file that she was married to a Traffic Division chap, although she never mentioned him. She ought to be safe from Newton's attention, he thought. He seemed to have a weakness for a pretty face. "Any luck with missing persons yet, DC Catchpole?" he asked.

"Not yet, sir, but I will keep trying. I want to keep the various stations on the ball to be aware." Peggy was keen to show that she was efficient and could be relied upon to get on with any task. True, this was a minor task, but she was ambitious and wanted to be noticed, and not because she was a woman. Since she had transferred over to CID from uniform, Peggy felt her male colleagues had treated her well. Maybe that was because she was older and more experienced now. She had the confidence to set her personal boundaries.

Webb and Newton had hardly settled back to their seats when DC Winter returned. Webb came to the door of his office. "How did you get on, Chris?" asked Newton.

"Well, there is only one CCTV camera in the area. I drove around to check there weren't any others and then got into the little supermarket as it opened at 8 am. They have a camera outside, pointing across their doorway, the pavement, the road and even a little bit of the pavement opposite. This tape I've got covers from 6 pm last night (when the manager changed it just before they closed) until this morning at just before 9 am when I got it from him."

"Well done! It sounds like you have some viewing to do! I should go through it in the side room – there's a machine in there," encouraged Newton.

"Note the time register of anyone, male or female, that walks towards the Recreation Ground from 6 pm onwards. Note any car registrations that you can pick up as well," instructed Webb, ensuring that the new man was adequately briefed. Then from 7:30 pm, note anyone or any car heading away from the field through until 10:30 pm. If you are unsure of anything, ask one of the others. Give your eyes a rest once in a while – it can be quite eye-watering, concentrating on usually fuzzy images for long periods. It can make you miss crucial small details."

"Yes, sir – I will do that!" confirmed DC Winter, pleased to have something to contribute to what for him was his first proper murder case.

"Right, I'll be off to check on that pub and anywhere else likely around there", informed Colin Newton, putting on his leather jacket and making for the door. He relished these opportunities to operate semi-independently.

DCI Webb climbed the stairs wearily to His Lordship's office, where he got agreement to pass a copy of the victim's face and clothing details to the press with a request for help in identifying him. "Let's get them to work for us for a change, instead of the other way around", was the instruction. "Let's get them to stop harassing us altogether", whispered Webb to himself as he descended the stairs again.

He typed up the press release, copied and pasted in the picture from the computer and sent it over to the media person for final approval and distribution. It was not the sort of job he felt he should be doing, and the bag of humbugs took a battering. It was almost pleasant to get a knock from DC Catchpole on the door to interrupt his thoughts. "Come in and tell me some good news!" he said, seeing a smile on her lips.

"I don't know if it is anything, but a farmer has made a missing person report. A man of twenty-two years old seems to have disappeared from a caravan he is renting. It is at Weatherall Farm, about 3 miles outside of Dinbourne, sir," she reported.

"Can you get out there straight away and check it out, please?" was the reply. "Yes, sir, straight away!" DC Catchpole was already keenly on her way

Over in Dinbourne, the dog walkers had long departed the re-opened field as the rain started to fall. Inevitably they had spent most of their time (in between managing the dogs) talking about the murder.

"Do they know who it was yet?" asked Sandra.

"No, I don't think so, although they will not release the name until he is formally identified, replied John knowledgeably.

"It's terrible that something happens somewhere like here: so close to home and the school", added Norma. "I'll not be able to look at that spot again without thinking of it."

"It is not the sort of thing you would normally associate with Dinbourne", commented Stan. "It's probably something to do with drugs", replied Louise sourly. "It generally is!"

"Has nobody seen Gilly this morning?" asked Jim, trying to appear casual. "Only she is generally here early with those rats on a string she walks", he added.

Sandra smiled to herself. Although he had never said anything, she had noticed that he generally watched Gilly with interest but appeared tongue-tied when she greeted him. "Maybe she thinks the place is still closed and taped off", she offered. "She comes from the other side of town, she told me, to walk those dogs."

Veronica hardly said anything other than 'Good morning' as she exercised the spaniels, but they noticed that she kept them well away from where the incident had taken place.

"I wish we could do something to help," said Stan ", but it is hard to know what."

"Keep your ears and eyes open, and pass anything on to the police", recommended Jim.

"Huh! For what good it will do," snorted John. "They are more interested in PR and statistics nowadays than catching criminals", he continued. "When I worked on the Suffolk Argus, people would sometimes tell us stuff, but if we passed it on, most times they ignored us!"

"That's a bit harsh", commented Jim. "It seems to me they do their best, but they're generally short on men and funding and always damned if they do or don't do a thing."

John used the excuse of Fi pulling away to avoid an argument from that rare person: someone who did not unthinkingly accept and agree with what he said. Gradually the rest of the group dispersed back across the field to their various homes.

DS Colin Newton pulled up outside the Cross Keys pub at just after 11 am when it opened, parking his car on Church Road. He ducked inside quickly to avoid the rain that had started an hour ago and found the landlord, Archie Weatherburn. He had a worn-out look and a slight Scots accent. Colin introduced himself. "Oh yes, one of the regulars said there was a stabbing down the road yesterday."

"Well, not exactly, but a man was killed. He produced the picture. "Have you seen this chap about?"

Archie wrinkled his nose, put his glasses on and peered at the piece of paper. "Um, I cannot be sure, but it looks like a young chap who calls in occasionally."

"Was he in on Monday night?" asked Colin eagerly.

"Yes, I think he was. The rugby was on satellite tv, and there were a dozen or so fellows in here. He sat watching it, nursing a pint for the whole match. I won't get rich off the likes of him, but every little bit helps. A dozen faces is good for a Monday here now. Some weeks I may as well close up at 9 pm."

"Was he sat with anyone else?" asked Newton, anxious to get him to focus on the victim.

"No, he sat over in the corner, minding his pint alone. The match started at 5:45, but I don't think he came in until after it had started. He is a quiet one and not a big drinker. Before you ask, I don't even know his name. He left as soon as the rugby finished at about 7:30 pm. So would I have done if I could – Scotland were thrashed by England, and it was a boring game."

"That's a shame," sympathised Newton. "Do you know where he lives or anything else about him?"

"No, I presume he is local. Visitors are more likely to head for a town centre pub rather than one on a housing estate. He has only come here occasionally for the last few months, and I think it has always been for the sport on satellite TV, so he has not got it at home, I guess."

"Well, thanks very much indeed for your help", replied Newton. "If you think of anything else, however small, could you let me know, please? Maybe show this picture to your regulars, see if they know his name or where he lives? Here's my card."

"So is he the poor fellow that got killed then?" asked Archie. Newton nodded. "Ah! Poor beggar, he didn't look the type to harm anyone else. Yes, I'll ask about, sure enough."

Newton left the pub pleased. He had established that the guy had arrived around 6 pm and left the pub at about 7:30 pm. It followed that now they knew from which direction he had approached the field. After swig or two of bottled water in his car, he drove the short distance up the road to the shops on the opposite side. The rain has stopped, and getting out, he saw the CCTV camera outside the little supermarket. DC Winter had interviewed there, but he said that it closed at 6 pm. He decided he would check the other shops as well.

Avoiding the puddles underfoot, he found that the hardware shop had closed at 5 pm; the hairdressers did not open on a Monday and having screened windows, the betting shop manager had not observed anything either. He had also closed at 6 pm. None of them had any CCTV pointing into the street, although the betting shop had one covering the counter. 'I wonder if there is a camera on that church, the far side of the field?' he wondered. Newton got back in his car and drove to it.

Getting out, he looked up for signs of a camera without success. He could see that there was a light on, though, so the church must be open. He didn't really like churches much and vicars even less as a breed, but he ventured inside in the interests of being thorough.

The vicar was just inside, slowly pulling out stacked chairs and arranging them into a small semi-circle. He wore a tweed jacket revealing a dog collar and black top. He was partly bald, probably in his fifties with a gaunt, grey face that suggested doom and hellfire more than 'All things bright and beautiful.' Hearing the squeaky door, he looked up from his task and gave a faint smile. Newton stepped forward and introduced himself.

"Ah, I expect that you are investigating the sad case across the road", he responded. "Such a terrible business."

"Yes", confirmed Newton, extracting a copy of the victim's picture to show him. Pausing and squinting through powerful glasses he removed from his pocket, the vicar slowly shook his head. "No, it is not anybody I have met around here yet. I have only been here about six months, though," he added apologetically. "Would you like me to keep a copy to show others?" he offered. "The confirmation class are here tonight – they may be nearer to the fellow's age group than most of the rest of the congregation. It is who I am setting the chairs out for – I like to make it as informal as possible," he beamed.

"That would be much appreciated, Reverend", replied Newton. "You don't have any CCTV?" he checked.

"No, there is no lead roof to be stolen. This church is too modern for that, and there is precious little of value inside either. It is normally locked when there is no service."

"Would anybody have been here yesterday evening?" questioned Newton, trying to get any slight lead from his visit.

"There used to be a Monday night choir practice, but they had all left or died by the time I was transferred here. The organist comes in to practice sometimes early Monday evening, but he is away skiing this week in Switzerland, lucky chap. I have to cover two other parishes and this one, so I doubt anyone will be in until the flower arranger next Saturday. Half a dozen ladies organise a rota between them for Saturday mornings, and a cleaner comes in the afternoon." Newton thanked the Vicar and left, and went back to his car, called the office and spoke to Webb, telling him his news. He then returned to Ipswich.

When he got back to the office, it seemed empty, until he realised they were all crowded into the side room, trying to see something on the computer monitor. The CCTV film had aroused their interest. It showed their man walking past at 7:38 pm, head down and hands in the pockets of his jacket, heading towards the Recreation Ground. However, nobody appeared to be following him, and very few people were on the video at all except for a couple of elderly females. There were a few cars, and their registration numbers had been noted after some difficulty with low-resolution images.

The next task was for DCs Winter and Gatesby to identify who owned the cars and contact them to determine whether they had seen anything and be aware that any of them could also be the suspected murderer. After several phone calls, they didn't learn anything of interest from them but added their names to the whiteboard; one was a young guy called David Burke from Ennis Avenue, visiting his girlfriend at 6:30 pm on the other side of town. He was seen returning at 11:34 pm. A call to the girlfriend confirmed his story. Two other vehicles were owned by older men claiming that they were returning home from work. Checks with their employers confirmed their accounts. Gale Toomey, a female agency home carer visiting a client on Summers Road amongst other scheduled calls, was the only other car driver. The agency confirmed that she was with the client between 7-9 pm with a second carer who was her passenger.

DC Catchpole reached the farmhouse and was greeted at the door by the farmer's wife, a hard-bitten looking woman who abruptly announced that she would call her husband on the radio. He arrived ten minutes later in a mud-splattered Range Rover that had seen better days. Apologising in advance if it was a waste of time, he invited her to jump into the vehicle. "Yours is likely to get bogged down on the lane", he explained. "There is a chap called Robert Howson, who does casual work for me around the place. He was supposed to help me fix a gate this morning but didn't turn up. He rents an old cottage from me, so I went over there to chase him up: he isn't on the phone. Anyway, I couldn't get a reply. We haven't got a spare key, so I couldn't go in."

"When did you last see him," asked DC Catchpole.

"Sunday morning," the farmer said. "He walked past our house at about elevenish. He was probably going up to the pub. He usually does that on a Sunday lunchtime."

The two-up, two-down cottage was somewhat ramshackle, and Peggy wondered what princely sum was taken as rent. They banged on the door, called out his name and looked through the downstairs windows without seeing any signs of life. "I think we are going to have to break in" decided Peggy aloud.

"Let me lass" offered the farmer gallantly and gave two hefty kicks to the back door with the sole of his welly boot." It flew open as easily as an Advent calendar.

"Police! Mr Howson, police entering!" shouted DC Catchpole. There was no response, and she cautiously entered a grubby back kitchen, followed at a distance by the farmer. A breakfast bowl and mug lay in the sink, and the small table was covered with a stained oilcloth. Venturing into the front room, a shabby armchair pointed at a little tv and a smoke-stained electric fire. A single light bulb hung overhead without a shade, decorated instead by cobwebs. An old dirty sheet hung against the window.

Calling out again, Catchpole mounted the narrow stairs, signalling her companion to stay downstairs. The wallpaper had long departed its decorative endeavour, probably in despair, and the handrail only seemed to have a tentative relationship with the wall. She pulled out a small torch as the light switch failed to yield results. The narrow beam showed a minute landing leading to a bathroom and two bedrooms. Pushing open the door to her left, she found it was empty, save for a couple of cardboard boxes. The bathroom was empty and emitted a stink. Closing its door with relief, she turned the handle to her right, slightly fearful of what she may find. A bed was piled high with blankets and spare clothes, presumably to give additional warmth. Poking them gingerly with her torch, to her relief, nobody was sheltering beneath them. Sighing, she called down, "Nobody here."

Descending the stairs, Catchpole was reunited with the farmer, looking both relieved and grateful. "Anywhere he may have gone to?" she asked. "No idea", was the reply.

As they stepped outside through the partly shattered backdoor, a muffled screech emitted from the Rangerover. It turned out to be the farmer's wife on the radio. Peggy could overhear most of the mainly one-sided conversation; Robert Howson had just turned up at the farmhouse. He had met someone (it sounded like 'filthy slut') at the pub on Sunday and gone home with them. Having stayed the last three nights, he had only just woken up, having overslept.

The journey back in the Range Rover was taken up with the farmer apologising profusely and repeatedly.

"Don't worry about it", re-assured Peggy. "You did the right thing, and at least we now know he is safe."

"No, we don't", he exclaimed. "We'd better get back as soon as we can. He is alone with my wife, and you may be needed to keep the peace!"

A rather pathetic looking man was indeed being harangued when they returned to the farmyard. "Mr Robert Howson?" checked DC Catchpole. The man nodded, grateful for any intervention. "Are you OK, sir?" she continued.

"Oh yes, thank you", he responded, his face lighting up. Before he could launch into a long time-wasting explanation, Catchpole turned to his boss. "Better get that back door fixed as soon as possible, eh?" He nodded her assent as she climbed back into her car. Giving a wave, she exited quickly.

'No point in getting involved in employment disputes on a murder enquiry,' she thought to herself as she headed back to HQ. Given the state of his home, she could hardly blame Robert Howson for accepting whatever hospitality he was offered elsewhere.

Having had his information from the pub confirmed, Newton felt at a bit of a loose end, so he got hold of the pile of witness statements to read properly.

The views expressed were all fairly standard stuff, recorded by a competent police constable. Still, DS Newton knew that occasionally 'the devil was in the detail', so he got a sheet of paper. He made a rough sketch of the Recreation Field and marked on the witnesses positions as they and other witnesses described them before and after Veronica Hedley had raised the alarm. They all seemed to correlate with what had been said, with no anomalies. Not all of the dog walkers had paid much attention to Gilly Wallis, the professional dog walker. This wasn't thought particularly suspicious by the officer who had phoned her since she was on the far side of the field from them.

He walked over to the copier, scanned the sketch into the file, and printed one copy out, which he fixed to the whiteboard. Whilst he was doing it, he mused that it didn't feel feasible that anyone could walk so close to a body without noticing it and, almost from habit, tapped the name Gillian Wallis into the police computer database.

She came up as the wife of Jeremy Wallis, currently serving three years in prison for a series of burglaries. Bringing the computerised case file up onto his screen, he could see that she had not been implicated. She had said that she believed that her husband was out working as a cleaner on the nights in question, as he had done so many other nights since becoming unemployed.

The investigating officer clearly had not believed her from his notes but had observed that she was not very supportive of her husband and seemed to have had a poor relationship with him before being arrested. He could not prove she was aware of his crimes, so she had walked free. She was shown as redundant at the time, so she had presumably started her dog walking business when money from her spouse dried up. If the victim knew something about Gilly, maybe she could have sought to shut him up? He would keep this witness in mind as someone worth examining again later.

Judging from the statements, the Constable had asked the same set of questions in the same order: Name, telephone number & address, email address, dog name and where were you on the field when Veronica shouted? What did you do then? Did you see or touch the body? When was the last time you visited or passed by the field? Did you see any other person or anything suspicious then? Newton opened a new page on his PC and inserted a table. He typed the witnesses names down the left-hand side. Then across the top header, he labelled the columns. In column 1, he typed 'position confirmed by another witness.' Column 2 was 'contact or sight of the body' and column 3 ', previous visit.' Finally, column 4 became 'who did you see?'

Colin then took each statement individually and filled in the columns. It was laborious, but he found that (a) it gave an order to random information in his mind, and (b) he could at least be seen to be doing something constructive. When he had completed the task, all of the witnesses had a tick in the first column. This suggested that they had either told the truth about where they were or that he was facing a massive if unlikely conspiracy.

Most of the witnesses saw only the body's feet protruding from the bush, except Veronica, whose dogs had found it, Jim who had gotten to her first and Stan checking for a pulse. Once again, other witnesses corroborated that. It was columns 3 and 4 that gave him pause for thought.

Everyone had been there on Monday morning, as was their habit, and had not noticed anything amiss. Gilly, Sandra, Veronica, and Stan said they did not go near the field again until Tuesday morning. John Westrup had said that he also visited again at about 2:30 pm on Monday, as his dog was hefty and needed more than one walk per day. He left before the children came out of school at 3:15 pm. Norma Livingstone said that she walked with Bella past the field and went to and from the school to pick up her children between 3 and 3:30 pm. She had noticed John And Fi leaving the area as she walked to the school along Masterson Road. She also saw a couple of Mums with their children on the swings on her way back.

Jim Coxall said that he sometimes exercised Rex a second time on the field in the afternoon but did not need to on Monday. He took the dog to work with him on Monday night, so he would get plenty more exercise there, patrolling around a large industrial site. He believed that he saw Veronica from a distance walking her pair of spaniels on his way to work in his car at around about 7:15 pm, but it was dark by then, so he couldn't be sure it was her. 'Or is he trying to divert attention, I wonder,' thought Newton. The job made one suspicious of every statement, however innocent-sounding.

Colin flipped back to Veronica's statement. There was no mention of her returning to the Recreation Ground at night. He remembered her pair of spaniels as the lively ones he kept clear of, leaping up and down with excitement. He was no expert on dogs (due to an unfortunate incident with a corgi when he was young) but guessed that they to would need a second bout of exercise per day to get rid of some of that energy. Was it her? He imagined that not too many people would have a pair of spaniels in the neighbourhood. Or had she simply forgotten? She was very distressed when they saw her, and she may have omitted to mention it through panic. He knocked on Ron Webb's door and entered at his nod. He told him his concerns about Veronica's statement. "You know I don't like loose ends and inconsistencies", Webb pronounced. "Go and see her now and ask her about it directly and watch her reactions, whether she is at home or work. I know she said that she does night shifts at the bakery."

"Right, sir, I will!" replied Colin. "There was also one other witness that may be worth talking to again. That professional dog walker woman Gilly. I was suspicious of her not noticing the body when she walked by it and looked her up. It turns out she is the wife of a convicted burglar who is currently inside. The investigating officer was suspicious of her, but there was no proof."

"Good work Colin," Webb said. You go and see this Veronica person, and I will visit Mrs Wallis. Maybe she just did not want to get involved with the police again," he added, and Jim left the office with a smile on his face. He headed straight back to Dinbourne.

It was about 5 pm by the time he pulled up outside Veronica Hedley's home. It was a small semi-detached thirties build on Kilburn Street. He rang the doorbell and heard excited barking behind it. There was a muffled call of 'wait a minute' and a pause. A startled Veronica eventually answered the door. "Sorry, I had shut the dogs in the kitchen", she greeted him. He held up his warrant card, and she let him into the living room, where they sat down. " Sorry, I recognise you now from the other time," she said.

"I hope that you have recovered a little since then", opened Colin. " I have a small point to clear up from the statement you gave to my colleague. Can you tell me again when was the last time you went to the Recreation Ground before last Tuesday morning?"

"It was Monday morning, about 9 o'clock, like I told the officer. I go there every weekday at about that time. Why?" she queried.

"Well, it's just that we had another witness who claims that they believe in having seen you and your pair of spaniels there on Monday night at about 7:15 pm. Can you explain that?"

"No, it couldn't have been me," said Veronica. "I would have been at work on the night shift from 6:30 pm."

"Do you know anyone else with a pair of spaniels in the area?" continued Colin.

" I haven't come across any", was the reply. "Hold on a minute", she added and called, "Carol! Can you come here a minute, please?"

A dark-haired woman in a red jumper and jeans entered the room, looking quizzical. Colin introduced himself. "I'm her partner", she explained. "What is it?"

"Carol, do you know of any other pair of spaniels around here?" asked Veronica.

"No, I have never come across even another single cocker spaniel or springer spaniel around here. We must be the only ones brave enough to take a pair of such loonies on!" Carol responded.

"Well, Carol, did you take your dogs out last Monday night?" asked Colin.

Carol looked a little uncomfortable and said, "Yes."

"Can you tell me what time that was and where you went, please?" said Colin.

"It was after my TV programme finished, which would make it just before 7 o'clock. I took them on their leads up to the Recreation Ground," admitted Carol.

"You promised you would not go up there in the dark!" exclaimed Veronica. "I worry about you! Why couldn't you go earlier while it was light?"

"It gets dark at around 4 o'clock, and I'm still working until 6 pm. Just because I work online from home doesn't stop Mr Arnold from checking up on me! We can't afford for me to lose this job," argued Carol. "You make too much fuss! I can look after myself, and I do have the dogs with me. I felt like chilling out to some TV before taking the dogs on Monday."

"Oh yes, two lovable mutts that will lick any attacker to death! That murder happened right there!" exclaimed Veronica vehemently, fighting back the tears with a catch in her throat.

"I wouldn't have been alone if you didn't work that damn night shift! I hardly get to see you during the week. When one of us is working, the other is sleeping and vice versa," Carol retaliated.

"Excuse me, ladies, but I seem to have caused upset enough here", ventured Colin, almost forgotten by the pair. "Carol, did you see anyone else hanging around when you were there?"

"Definitely not", replied Carol, a little more calmly, "nor anything else suspicious. I was quite alone, and I kept the dogs on the lead in case they ran off in the dark."

"Thank you, and sorry to have caused an upset. I will see myself out," responded Colin feeling unequal to refereeing a domestic dispute between two females. As he walked back to his car, he reflected on why Veronica might not have wanted a police officer or fellow dog walker to walk her back to her home after her discovery. Some people like to keep their private lives to themselves.

As Colin left the house, DCI Webb was just pulling up outside the home of Gilly Wallis. It was a rented semi on the opposite side of Dinbourne. There was a neat front garden and a sound of barking when he knocked on the door. Gilly answered with a surprised look on her face, holding onto the collar of a Dalmation called Millie. "I spoke to a policeman on the phone earlier today," she said. "Is this about that or my husband?"

"No, it is about the incident at the Recreation Area", assured Webb. "May I come in, please?"

"Yes, you better had. It's cold out there," Gilly replied. The living room was chilly, sparsely furnished, and she sat on a rather beaten up looking sofa. Millie, the dalmation, jumped up beside her, and Gilly put a protective arm around her as she sat tensely on the edge of the seat. Millie responded by occasionally giving Gilly a lick to her ear. DCI Webb lowered himself onto a plain wooden chair beside an old table with stain rings where hot dishes had been left on it.

"I understand that you were at the recreation Ground this morning, Mrs Wallis?" Webb said.

"Yes, I go there every weekday morning. I pick up four customers dogs from different houses nearby in my car and leave the motor at the last one in Talbot Road. After the walk, I put the other three in the car and drop them off back to their houses before heading back in this direction. Then I pick up some more to walk on the field up the road from here, together with Millie. I haven't been running 'Walkies' long, but I already have quite a few regular customers, plus some casual extras."

"Good, that explains a bit. Do you keep the dogs on a lead on the Recreation Field, or do you let them off?" asked Webb.

"Oh no, I never let any client's dogs off the lead in case they ran off or had an accident. The only one who walks off lead is Millie here when we get to the local field, but she is well trained and always responds to commands, don't you, girl," she responded, stroking the dogs head.

"So do you get to see all the owners when you are fetching and dropping off their dogs?"

"Not exactly", responded Gilly. "I have a few disabled or elderly customers, so I usually see them when I call. Some people get me to walk their dogs while they are out at work all day. They give me a key to let myself in, and I put down food and water at some of those homes."

"Can you tell me about what time you finished walking dogs on Monday then, please, approximately Mrs Wallis?" continued DCI Webb.

"About 4:30 pm by the time I had dropped the last one off and come back here for a bite to eat with Millie," said Gilly confidently.

"And did you go out after that?" enquired Webb.

"Yes, I did. Mr & Mrs Shelley had asked me to dogsit Dilly the daschund on Monday night. They are both disabled, so I usually walk their dog in the morning with the others on the Recreation Ground. They had been invited to a birthday party on Monday night, and Dilly gets separation anxiety: she chews the furniture and barks continuously if she is left.

I got there just before 8 pm, in time for their taxi to pick them up and left at just after 11 pm when they returned. Dilly was no trouble with me being there, so I sat and read a book and watched some television. Sorry, I'm rambling on. I don't have many people to talk to who can answer back," she added, embarrassed.

"Not at all", reassured Webb, glad that she was talkative. It made his job easier and meant that he didn't have to ask so many questions. "Was it far from here?" he queried.

"The other side of town – 263 Summers Road."

"OK, the other thing I am curious about is how it was that you never noticed the body sticking out from the bushes up at the Recreation Ground?" Webb added as casually as he could.

"Thinking about it since the other policeman telephoned on Tuesday, I am pretty sure that I was on my mobile phone. Some customers ring me to re-arrange times later on, but being early, I am sure that is when I kept trying to ring Mills Solicitors. It was engaged for a long time. Between that, keeping the four dogs from tangling up their leads and clearing up after them, I was probably not paying much attention to my surroundings."

"Ringing the solicitors, you say," said Webb, his curiosity aroused. "Are you in some sort of trouble?"

"Oh no, not really. I was trying to get an appointment for this morning to sort out a divorce. I got an appointment for 9:15 am and took the dogs out a little later. I cannot afford to miss them out – I need the money.

I am guessing that you know about my husband, Robbie. People don't believe me when I say that I didn't know what Robbie was doing, but I really didn't. It wasn't a good marriage, and he was always having a go at me. He gave me a black eye last Christmas time after he got the sack from the factory. Some money went missing, and they hadn't got any proof, but they got rid of him anyway. He told me he didn't do it but seemed to have more money in his pocket than usual. When I called him a liar, he hit me. That was the final straw for me, and I started looking for a way out. Of course, he couldn't get a decent reference from the factory. Then he got some casual shifts working nights for a contract cleaning company. He hated it, and money was tight. I also worried that he might steal from one of the offices because he was often expected to work alone.

I had been made redundant from the travel agents – too many people booking holidays online nowadays. When I found out from the police about the burglaries, it was the end for me with him. I couldn't trust him ever again after all those lies. It was some of the nights he had told me he was out cleaning. I just wanted to make a fresh start, and starting 'Walkies' is helping."

"Yes, I can understand that, Mrs Wallis," said Webb sympathetically. "You must know that we have to follow these things up?"

"Oh, yes," she replied. "I understand that."

"Then, hopefully, I will not have to bother you any further. Goodbye, Mrs Wallis and to you too, Milly." Milly wagged her tail.

Before Webb drove away, he made a note himself: check that Wallis went to Mills Solicitors Wednesday morning and check Mr & Mrs Shelley of 263 Summers Road for that dogsitting alibi. Timings important, he underlined. If she had got there at 8 pm, as she said, she still had time to do a murder first close by on the Recreation Field. It was only about a five-minute drive.

His detective's eyes had also taken in one other detail almost unconsciously when he had followed Gilly Wallis into her home: she was only an inch or two shorter than himself, which made her between 5 feet 10 to 5 feet 11 inches tall. It was quite tall enough to bring a weapon down on the head of the diminutive victim. It had been difficult to judge at the murder site, but the pathologist had said that the man was only 5 feet 6 inches.

As he drove back to Ipswich, Webb wondered about a possible motive? To silence the young man from telling something he knew about her or her possible involvement in the burglaries? That was entirely possible since he only had her word for her innocence. Was it love? She was trying to get a divorce. What if she and Cosby had been lovers? She was older but still attractive. It would hinder her story of being the 'innocent party' in a divorce. Her husband could counter-claim that he had been wronged as well and was entitled to half of their belongings.

Then there was the missing wallet: there was no rule that said that muggers had to be male, especially when they were much larger and more desperate than the victim. 'Money or sex – the two major reasons for most crimes' was the old adage as accurate now as it had been when Moss joined the police force over thirty-five years ago. Moss felt his stomach rumble. 'Another heated up late dinner', he reflected. 'Oh well, at least I have someone making my meal', he thought.

Chapter 4. Morning of Thursday 8th Dinbourne.

Jim Coxall locked his front door and commanded "heel" to the excited Rex. She walked obediently on his right side beside the fence as they carried on up Summers Road. He wondered how many of the other regular dog walkers would be on the Recreation field this morning? He enjoyed the little bit of social contact it gave him. That was something he particularly missed – the banter with his mates in the Army. Security work was usually quite solitary, and he wasn't due back to the company he was currently working for until 6 pm. His boots set a measured pace that he had long been conditioned into, and his black and tan Doberman friend matched it at his side without pulling on the lead.

His thoughts were jolted by Rex's need to stop and cock his leg up against a hedge that still had a topping of frost. Paused just there, he saw a glint amongst the branches. At first, he thought it was some discarded litter, but looking closer, he could identify the case of a mobile phone. There was something else near to it as well, black and square. Jim didn't know if they were connected to yesterday morning, but his Military Police background had not deserted him. He pulled a clean poo bag out of his pocket and reached through the branches and twigs. He captured the phone and got the back of his hand scratched by twigs for his trouble. The disturbance had caused the other object to fall further down the bush, and he could now see that it was a wallet. It was hard to reach from where he stood, so he led Rex around to the other side of the hedge and stooped to retrieve it with a new bag from near the bottom of the hedge. Looking up, he could see that it was the house that had been empty for some time, with the curtainless windows and overgrown garden. He crammed his finds in their bags into the pockets of his combat jacket. Soon Rex was walking with him across into Talbot Road and through the entrance of the white-topped field.

As he entered, Gilly Wallis was about to exit with her four charges. They immediately started yapping at Rex like a bunch of catty schoolgirls. The racket was beneath Rex's dignity, so he merely summonsed a single sonorous low, loud 'woof' from deep within his chest and stood with his muzzle in the air, pointedly ignoring them. "Good morning!" Jim ventured over the noise of the dogs. "I missed your smiling face yesterday morning. Are you OK?"

Gilly smiled back. "Yes, I'm fine. I had booked a morning off to sort out some stuff. Back to the old routine today, though. The police contacted me about the dead man. I must have walked past him, completely oblivious. My mind was probably on other matters, I guess."

"Yes, that will be it", Jim replied, thinking of her frequent phone use. He was still beating himself up a couple of minutes later for not thinking of something better to say to her before she departed. Still, it was progress: it was the most extended conversation he had managed with her alone since he first saw her a couple of months ago. He liked her independent air and fresh-faced look and the way she wrinkled her nose when smiling. Maybe one day, it would lead to a date, but he would have to summon up the courage to ask her out first. He had long ago noticed the absence of a wedding ring, but that didn't mean she hadn't got a partner. (He was not privy to the gossip of Stan and Louise.) He, the once confident soldier! His old mates would be taking the mick out of him if they could see him now, being so bashful! Across the field, Sandra took it all in, smiling secretly to herself.

Gilly carried down Talbot Road on the way to drop off Ronan the Pekinese. She smiled to herself that Jim wanted to talk to her and was aware that he was attracted to her. It was good to know that she was still attractive to someone after the long years with Robbie. Now that Robbie was in prison for burglary, she had spent yesterday morning visiting a solicitor to start divorce proceedings. Gilly certainly wasn't interested in starting another relationship yet, but it gave her hope for the future. That Jim seemed a straightforward sort of guy and clearly loved his dog a lot. She would never trust anyone like Robbie again, who didn't really like dogs.

Inevitably Stan and Louise were quizzing everyone else as to whether they knew any more about the crime. John was holding forth with a sense of superiority: "My reporter friend says that they have got a picture of the victim's face for the Friday edition of the Suffolk Argus. Maybe someone will recognise who it is then because the police haven't got a clue!" Noticing Jim arriving and remembering their disagreement yesterday, he walked the hairy Fi away.

Sandra was talking to Veronica about the best way to get dog hairs off clothes and carpets. She deliberately avoided talking about the murder with her unless she raised it herself because she had seemed quite upset by it. Norma arrived, turning her collar up against the cold, with black-haired Bella who made straight for her friend James the Golden Labrador. They sniffed each other and wagged tails as usual whilst the humans greeted each other less personally.

"Look!" said Jim, pulling the two clean poo bags out of his pocket. "I found these dumped in a hedge on the way here this morning: a wallet and mobile phone. Do you reckon they are connected with the crime?"

"Could be?" said Stan, moving closer and extending his palm. Let's see."

"No, I don't want to get fingerprints on them – that why I picked them up in bags", Jim explained. "Anyway, I'm going to hand them into the police station after I have taken Rex home."

"I certainly wouldn't want to handle them!" said Norma, disgusted. "It makes me shudder, thinking that someone might have robbed them out of the dead man's pockets!"

"If it was a robbery, why throw them away?" queried Jim. "Unless they just emptied the wallet and got rid of it."

"Did you spot a name?" demanded Louise. "I might have known him from the surgery."

"No, I'll leave that to the police. They will not want us interfering," responded Jim.

"Yes, I think that is the right thing to do", re-assured Sandra.

Offended at not being privy to its secrets, Louise said, "Come on, Stan, I'm getting cold standing here" and started heading for the gate. The rest also dispersed and returned to their homes.

Having given the dog a good run, it was about 10 am before Jim returned home, fed Rex and had a cup of tea and a piece of toast. Rather than doze in the armchair as he often did while on night duties, he then drove into the town centre in his beaten-up Ford Fiesta and hunted for a parking space near the small police station. Entering, he waited behind someone showing their license and insurance to the desk sergeant before being seen.

He handed over the two bags and explained why he suspected they might be connected with the murder. It seemed to make sense to the Sergeant who thanked him, took his details, and promised to ring the CID Serious Crime Squad immediately. It was just before 11 o'clock when Jim took the call. He told DCI Webb that he would go over there straight away to collect the finds. "It could be a real break!" he said excitedly as he left.

"Hmm! I'll believe it when I see it", growled Webb but hoped for better.

Jim was back by 2 o'clock, and Ron Webb accompanied him to the forensics lab. "I know people are always saying it, but these definitely are top priority – part of a murder enquiry we are stumped on," said Ron. Can you check them for prints to start with?" he asked. The Crime Scene Investigator's technician reluctantly agreed but sensed that it was necessary. He took the phone out of the bag with tweezers and held it under a UV light. "It's been wiped", he announced, then sniffing added, "some sort of alcohol-based product, I would guess." Giving up on prints, he pressed 0 four times, and the screen lit up. "Wonderful!" he exclaimed. "Finally, someone who never changed the factory preset entry code. I'll give it to Richard to download onto a computer, then email it to you. He will be back from lunch shortly. Let's have a look at the wallet. The wallet also failed to glow for him on the outside, but he still handled it with care when he opened it. "The original owners DNA may be caught on the insides of the compartments. Let me just swab each one." Having done that, he extracted a bank card and a Students Union membership card. They did show up partial fingerprints. "I will get them recorded and checked against the victim. The chances are they are his. It looks as if this is the bank card of a 'Mr. G. Crosby' and the Students Union card is for Cambridge University for last year and says 'Graham Crosby.' There is an ID photo on the Students Union card. Does that look like your victim?"

The two officers examined it, and both agreed that this was their man. "Well, at least we have a name now", commented Newton.

There was also a small head and shoulders photo of a young woman behind a plastic window, but no name. It looked a bit creased around the edges as if it had been taken out of the wallet a few times. "Maybe a girlfriend?"

ventured Newton. She looks about the same age." Webb nodded.

Jim took some pictures of the cards and photo onto his phone to have a quick reference for the details while the lab continued their investigations. "Thanks very much indeed!" said DCI Webb. "I owe you a drink!"

"If I collected all the drinks I am owed, from all the officers I have had promises from, I could be drunk for a year", replied the technician cynically.

"Ah, that is precisely why we must never let you have them then", quipped Colin as he exited laughing. Even Ron grinned. Returning to the office, Colin emailed the pictures to Will to record on the case notes and print up for the whiteboard and himself. He got the marker pen and wrote "Graham Crosby" under the forensics photo. The team swivelled their chairs to face the boss for a quick informal update.

"So what is a Cambridge Uni student doing in lovely Dinbourne midweek during term time then?" asked Peggy. "I'm guessing his original home is maybe there?"

"Good question, but the card is for last academic year, so he may have left in summer but kept it in his wallet. We should be able to find out by contacting the Admissions office there. Maybe you could get onto that in a minute, please DC Catchpole?" asked DCI Webb.

"The banks can be a bit cagey about letting out details", stated Chris. "Would you like me to pop down to the local branch before they shut to get his address and bank statement in person?"

"That would be excellent, thank you, and don't forget to get details of any Direct Debits or regular payments in. They may give us a local address," explained Webb.

DC Gatesby, could you see if he is on the Telephone Directory or Electoral Roll here or in Cambridge, please? He may not have re-registered if he has only recently left university. Maybe you could also canvass the local GP Surgeries and see if he is registered with one as well."

"Yes, Boss", he replied smartly.

"Right, Newton, meet me here at 8 am tomorrow. We will probably need to go up to Cambridge to make enquiries.

DC Will Gatesby found that the GP surgery lines were closed until tomorrow morning. Graham Crosby did not feature on the latest Electoral Roll or telephone directory, here or in Cambridge. "Blinking mobile phones!" he exclaimed. He ordered up copies of Electoral Rolls for two years ago when he was probably first old enough to enter onto it. It would not be available until the morning, so Gatesby wrote up his notes and checked to see if another old case he was involved with would get to court this week as previously planned. Unsurprisingly it had been adjourned for yet another month awaiting psychiatric reports, so he left for the day.

DC Peggy Catchpole was left waiting for ages listening to inane music on several university telephone lines until she found someone that could help her. Yes, a Graham Crosby had been registered as a student at St. Gabriel's College, but any further information could not be divulged without the presentation of a police warrant card. She gave DS Newton the information, and having not heard of the particular college before, he did a little bit of internet research into its location and other details.

DC Chris Winter managed to see an official at the bank, who seemed a bit flustered at his request and a bank card's photocopy. He was told that they would have to contact the manager for approval due to the Data Protection Act. "Fair enough", replied Chris. "Off you go then."

"Oh no, we don't have a manager on the premises very often. Those days are long gone. We have department heads, but they don't have the authority. Can you wait here while I make a phone call, please?" requested the lady.

Chris duly waited about twenty minutes but was eventually ushered through the security door where he could see the name, address, date of birth and recent statements on screen. He was allowed a print out when he had signed to say that they would only be shown to police officers. He asked a few details about the Direct Debits, which turned out to be for utility bills, mobile phone and house insurance. The account address was for a flat in Cambridge, but there was no recent rent paid or a mortgage. "People often move around without moving their account – you'd be surprised" was the response. Guessing that everyone would have departed from the office by now, Chris also knocked off for the night.

Chapter 5. Friday 9th October, Dinbourne.

The usual dog walkers were out in force at 9 am. John Westrup had brought a copy of that morning's Suffolk Argus he had bought on the way there. Battling to stop it blowing away on the wind, he showed the front page, emblazoned with the headline 'Mystery Man Murder: do you know who this is?' The story was written up like crusading journalism: 'This paper will help bring justice to Dinbourne!' 'Ring our hotline now if you can help!' and similar phrases. There was very little detail in it because the police didn't know much when they had gone to press.

Jim openly scoffed at it, trying to ape the nationals and sensationalising a sad event. Norma said she didn't want to look because it continued to be upsetting, which her husband said was bad for her. Gilly took a glance but declared it was nobody that she recognised. Veronica thought it didn't much look like what she saw. Sandra said that the face was slightly familiar. However, she also said that he looked like lots of other young men, so she was probably mistaken. Louise gave a bit of a start: "he looks like a chap that came to the Health Centre a few times", she declared. "I can't think of his name, but it will come to me eventually."

Meanwhile, DCI Webb and DS Newton were parking in an extravagantly priced 'pay & display' carpark near St. Gabriel's College, Cambridge.

To prove he had done some research, Newton told his boss that it was principally known for Languages and Politics studies, so St Gabriel as the patron saint of communication was entirely appropriate. "Politicians communicating?" Pull the other one, son. They only ever listen to themselves," corrected Webb sarcastically. "Didn't you watch the General Election this year?"

The building wasn't one of the ancient edifices attractive to tourists in the centre of Cambridge. It was situated on the city's edge in a red brick and concrete monolith resembling a seventies office block. After some confusion at the reception desk, they were finally directed to Professor Mason on the second floor. He wasn't aware that they were calling but said that he hadn't got to take a tutorial until 10 am. He had a slightly shabby tweed suit and lounged back in his armchair.

"I understand that you were the tutor of Graham Crosby, sir?" opened Webb after introductions and showing his warrant card.

"Yes, unfortunately, he dropped out of the course in his second year last May."

"Can you tell us why that was, please?"

Prof Mason looked over the tops of his spectacles in a confidential manner. "Well, although he worked quite hard initially, it all went to pieces. He asked to go back home when his Grandmother died. I understand that she had brought him up, and he was distraught. He returned a couple of weeks later, but it seems that a girl he was rather besotted with dumped him for another student. It isn't uncommon for this sort of thing to happen to students of his age. After that, he failed to attend lectures, tutorials, or to hand in work. We had a discussion, and he told me that he couldn't cope and was leaving. I tried to dissuade him, but his mind was made up. It was a pity because he was bright and may have been able to catch up with the course."

DS Newton pulled out a copy of the girl's photograph from the wallet and showed it to Prof. Mason. "Is this the girl?" he asked.

"Yes, although her hair is a bit different now. Her name is Madeline Elliott."

" Can you tell me where she lives?"

"No, I don't know. Madeline is one of my tutor group, but we don't keep addresses. I doubt whether I would be allowed to hand it over even if I did know it."

"Maybe we should make ourselves a little clearer, Professor", intervened Webb. "This is a murder investigation. We believe that he is the young man murdered in Dinbourne earlier this week, and we know very little about him."

"Oh, how dreadful! The poor chap. That puts things in a different light. I will ring down to reception to let you have her address and telephone number."

"Could you ask them to supply the addresses they have for Graham Cosby as well, please? The one for here in Cambridge and his home address."

"Yes, indeed, anything we can do to help. I think from what I gathered from our chat, Grandmother was leaving him her house so that he was returning there."

"What sort of chap was he?" Webb continued.

"Quiet, inoffensive, naturally good with languages but not very confident. Crosby seemed quite depressed towards the end of his studying here."

"Was it modern languages he was studying then?" asked Newton.

"Yes, combined with politics. Crosby was interested in the Balkan states. That's about all I can say about him, gentlemen, I'm afraid. Despite being in my tutor group for nearly two years, he wasn't the sort of chap that you got to know terribly well."

"So no obvious enemies then?"

"No, I doubt whether the majority of students even noticed him. As far as the girlfriend goes, I think that the vernacular phrase 'punching above his weight' probably applied."

Webb thanked him, and the Professor started to ring the reception to give them the requested information. As they walked back down the corridor, Newton glanced at his notebook. "We seem to be making progress, sir", he commented.

"Yes, we may know him a bit better now, but it makes it even harder to understand why someone wanted to kill him." They retraced their steps to reception and waited while a distinctly put-out receptionist slowly obtained and handed over the details requested.

Outside back in the car, Webb put the address of Madeline Elliott into the SatNav. It was less than 2 miles away, so he decided that they should try there next, even if she might be in lectures.

It turned out to be a house shared by four students, and she answered the doorbell. "What is it about?" she asked on the doorstep, looking at their warrant cards suspiciously. She was tall with dishevelled blonde hair, an oversize man's rugby shirt acting as a skirt and black tights. She looked as if she might have just got up: she was clutching half a mugful of black coffee and wasn't wearing any make-up.

"If you can let us in, please, it is something you may prefer to discuss in private", suggested Newton. Reluctantly she led the pair to an untidy communal room and slumped down on a dirty sofa, curling her legs beneath her. Newton moved some magazines and notebooks off a couple of wooden chairs, and they sat opposite her. They had previously agreed that Newton should lead the interview since he was nearer to the young woman's age group.

"I understand that you used to know a student called Graham Cosby. Can you tell us about him, please, love?"

"Don't 'love' me! she retorted. "Hasn't the police got any further than a patriarchy yet?"

"My sincere apologies Ms Elliott. I didn't mean to be offensive," apologised Newton.

"He was a bit of a saddo, really", Madeline continued without acknowledging him. "We were in the same tutor group, and I missed a lecture or two. He offered to let me copy his notes. I had problems understanding his handwriting, so he came around and even helped me understand it. After that, he sort of latched onto me, and we did go out a few times together. I found him a bit wet, though, easily upset and not a lot of fun. He hardly ever had more than one pint and wasn't into anything else. He obviously loved me a lot more than I loved him, and things drifted on for a bit. Then his granny got ill and died, and he went home for a couple of weeks. He had told me that she'd brought him up since he was young, and he hadn't got much other family. I don't think he ever got over it and went to pieces: he came back for a while but just stayed in his bed all the time. I was seeing someone else by then and eventually found out he had left the course. Anyway, what has he done wrong? Why do you want to know about him?"

Adopting a more serious tone, Newton addressed her in the way he had been taught to break the bad news: "I am very sorry to have to tell you that he has been murdered. I am sorry for your loss. We are trying to find out about his contacts. Did he have any enemies here?"

The disinterested cocky, and defensive persona seemed to fade from her face. "That is horrible! Do you know who did it? He was such a gentle sort; I cannot imagine anyone hating him, let alone killing him."

"We have no leads at present, Ms Elliott", concluded Newton. She raised a crumpled tissue to her eye, and as it seemed that there was nothing more to be learnt from her, they left.

On the way back to Ipswich, Newton commented on her. "The tissue didn't fool me. There were no real tears. She had dumped him for someone more fun. Still, it confirms what we heard from the tutor, doesn't it?"

"Some people feel that it is expected of them to show grief, even if they don't feel it. It's a sort of expected social behaviour, I suppose," responded Ron. He took another humbug from the bag and unwrapped it with his teeth whilst driving. He didn't offer one to Colin. He had learnt that they were always refused with an accompanying speech about 'keeping healthy and trying to lose some weight.' He knew that Colin also went to the gym two or three times a week. Health and fitness seemed to be a new religion, but he was convinced in Ron's case, the gym was a way of making himself more attractive to women as well as meeting them. His thoughts were confirmed when they stopped for some lunch before returning to Ipswich. He had ordered a tasty cottage pie whilst Ron had picked at a chicken salad.

It was mid-afternoon when they got back to the office, and various team members had stuff to report, so a meeting was convened so that they could all acquaint themselves with new information. DCI Webb gave a precis of the information they had gleaned in Cambridge, and DS Newton updated the whiteboard with the names and addresses from his notebook.

DC Chris Winter had examined the bank's statements and gave them a quick run-down on

Crosby's financial position: the account was still held at a branch in Cambridge. He paid electricity, gas, water, mobile phone, council tax and tv license for 73, Church Road, Dinbourne. That was the same address obtained from Cambridge. He had about £300 in his account but owed £18,000 student loan. He owned the house outright but didn't appear to be having any wages paid into the bank account. He occasionally banked £50, so he must be getting money from somewhere and was not receiving benefits. Could he be working somewhere cash in hand?

DC Will Catesby had received a couple of phone calls. One was from one of the dog walk witnesses called Louise Bennett. She recognised the face in the paper as Graham Crosby. She didn't have his address, but he had been a patient at the Health Centre, where she used to work. He had finally managed to contact them after hanging on in a telephone queue for half an hour, and they confirmed that a Graham Crosby was on their register. They wouldn't confirm an address without a personal call or an officially headed police letter.

The other call was from a reporter at the Suffolk Argus. As a result of their article, three people had contacted them with the same suggestion: the name was unknown, but all three said it looked like a chap who served on the till at Main

Road Petrol Station. "Could be where he is getting paid in cash", Will added. He had thanked the reporter but told him that he could not give him a quote.

DC Peggy Catchpole reported no appropriate sounding missing person's reports. The university had also called her to check that Webb and Newton were who they said they were. "Bet it was that sour-faced receptionist", speculated Newton.

"OK, thank you, everybody, for your efforts, but we mustn't let up", instructed Ron Webb. Tomorrow I would like DC Gatesby to call upon the Health Centre and determine why our man was referred. Was he on any medication? The autopsy didn't show any.

Secondly, I'd like DC Catchpole and DC Winter to visit the home address. Book the key out from the evidence box. Gather up anything relevant – papers, medication – you know the drill. If the key doesn't work, you have my permission to break in, but make sure you check that nobody else has done so before us.

Thirdly, DS Newton, I think you and I had better make one more trip out today to that petrol station. Anything else, folks? Right, I have a couple of phone calls to make. I will see you tomorrow."

Firstly Webb called Mills Solicitors. They were happy to confirm that a Mrs Wallis had attended an appointment with them on Wednesday morning.

After having difficulty finding a telephone number for Mr & Mrs Shelley of 263 Summers Road (since it was ex-directory), the dogsit customers confirmed that the 'lovely Gilly had indeed looked after their naughty Dilly on Monday night. She had been on time so that their taxi could pick them up at 8 pm.' "Damn" was all Ron could say to himself, but she still wasn't eliminated. He only had her word that she wasn't involved in the burglaries and could have committed the murder on her way there.

Chapter 6. Friday 9th October, Dinbourne.

5 pm.

It was about 5 pm by the time Webb and Newton reached the Main Road Petrol Station in Dinbourne. Ron could see that the forecourts four pumps were all busy, so he decided to stop short of it on the opposite side of the road. The petrol station had a wide frontage, but to the shop's right were air and water machines and then a hand car-wash operation that appeared to be still busy.

The pair of them walked through the shop (mainly selling sweets, sandwiches, newspapers, alcohol and cigarettes) to the cashier at the far end. He was a rather acne-ridden youth in his late teens sporting a Ramones rockband teeshirt and greasy looking hair. "Hello, is the manager about, please?" asked Colin.

The chap picked up a phone and said, "I will ring through. He's out the back. Who shall I say it is? He won't see reps at this time of day, though."

"No, we are the police", assured Colin, flashing his warrant card.

A tall, bearded man appeared and invited them to his office. It was a tiny cubicle with clipboards full of papers hanging from the walls, an overflowing 'IN' tray and a bin stuffed with fast food packaging and sandwich boxes. He didn't appear to be in urgent need of a meal from his expanding waistline anytime soon. He introduced himself as Norman Bell and sat in the only chair, leaving the two police officers to cram themselves in standing.

"Is this your petrol station Mr Bell?" asked DCI Webb.

"No, I manage it for Colin Burwell. He has another petrol station on the other side of town and the MiniMart on the Square."

"Do you employ a chap called Graham Cosby?" Webb continued.

"Um, well, we have had him as a casual worker for the last month or two covering some shifts", replied Burwell.

"When did you see him last?"

"Monday. I saw him leave at 6 pm when he handed over. I stay until about 7 pm to catch the late customers before locking up. It's only worth staying open until 10 o'clock tonight and Saturday."

"When was Graham due in next then?"

"He had got Tuesday and Wednesday off because he had worked at the weekend, but was due in yesterday. He never showed up or even gave us a phone call, so I had to fill in. I couldn't get a reply from his phone either, so I expect he is avoiding me. That's the trouble with casual staff: they are unreliable and always coming and going. Maybe he's found a better-paid job somewhere, or maybe he couldn't be bothered." Bell finished this statement in an indignant tone, whilst Newton furiously scribbled down notes.

"I guess he will not get paid then. How are casual cashiers paid, Mr Bell?"

"They're on the national minimum wage per hour for each shift they do. I input it onto the payroll programme at the weekend. That does the deductions and prints out a wage slip. I stick that into an envelope with the right amount of cash from the till. They get it next time they are here. What's this all about then?"

"I see that you sell newspapers here, Mr Bell. Have you read today's Suffolk Argus?" Webb continued as if butter wouldn't melt in his mouth.

"No, I haven't! I don't get time with all the jobs I have to cover. Merchandising, invoices, charging 5p for carrier bags, checking in deliveries, cleaning: you name it!"

"Well, the face of Graham Cosby was on the front page of every one of the Suffolk Argos you checked into deliveries. I'm surprised you didn't notice him."

"Why, what's he done?"

DCI Webb leaned forward, looming very close over Bells face. "What he has done is that he got himself murdered! Any ideas about why that could be?"

"No, I haven't. He left here alright last Monday, bang on time. He said he was going to watch the rugby on TV at a pub."

"Ah, timing. I'm sure you'd like to help us, so can we have your CCTV footage from last Monday, please? I see that one camera points out across the forecourt, so that should verify your story, shouldn't it?"

"Why didn't you say so before then, instead of all these questions? Of course, you can have the recordings for Monday." He opened a desk draw and rummaged inside. "There!" he exclaimed triumphantly, producing it. Colin held open an evidence bag and let him drop the recording into it.

"Thank you very much indeed for your help Mr Burwell," said DCI Webb pleasantly. They left and walked back into the shop. Webb selected a bag of humbugs off the rack and paid the spotty youth.

When the pair got back to the car up the road, DCI Webb turned to Newton instead of driving straight off and asked: "How do you think that went then?"

"You certainly made him nervous, sir. He was sweating, and his body language was all about lies. He kept glancing up to the right. I don't reckon he would have been so eager to give us the CCTV footage without thinking it was for his benefit either."

"Very good", approved Webb. "I also watched you avoid handling the tape in case we wanted a copy of his prints as well!" Newton didn't have to answer. He just gave a broad cheeky grin and held a thumb up. "Right, time to go home," said Ron, reaching for the ignition key.

"Wait a minute, sir, please. I think I know the man who just came out of the shop," blurted Newton. They watched the man walk across the forecourt. His face was lit up enough to see him more clearly. "Sneaky Sid!" whispered Newton. "I thought he was still inside. Look, he's crossing and coming our way. Turn your face my way in case he recognises us." DCI Webb didn't ask why. Years of experience told him to do it and ask questions afterwards.

They waited until Sid was past the car before Newton quietly opened his car door and crept silently after him. Reaching forward, he put a hand on his shoulder from behind. "Evening Sid. Enjoying some fresh air?"

Turning and scowling when he saw who it was, Sid rasped, "And no thanks to you, pig!" DCI

Webb had caught them up and stood to his other side in case he wasn't up for helping the police with their enquiries. "Given that you are probably still on parole and I would be failing in my duty not to ask you questions, what were you doing over at the petrol station? Catching up on the exorbitant price of fuel these days? Or nicking stuff from the shop?"

"I haven't nicked anything – I paid for it. I bought some fags."

"So let's check your pockets, shall we? Nothing sharp, dangerous or naughty in them, is there?" He reached into the jacket pockets and pulled out a packet of cigarettes and an old lighter. His jeans pockets contained a wallet with a £5 note in it. "No receipt for the cigarettes then. It is not looking good. Newton pulled out a small torch he kept in his jacket and shone them on the cigarettes. "Oh, no wonder. These are the sort without any tax paid on them, from abroad." He pulled out an evidence bag and dropped them in. "Right, it's only one packet, and I don't want to be hard on you, so we'll make a deal: you keep your mouth shut and don't go back to buy any more. In return, I won't arrest you and get you sent back to prison for breaking parole by buying iffy fags!"

"Alright", growled Sid. "You have my word."

"Not a word though, Sid", emphasised Newton. "I've got a witness here, and I could still come back and charge you if I hear that you've been blabbing. Now mess off back to your hovel!"

The two detectives walked back to the car again, well pleased with their night's work. "Hooky cigarettes," said Webb in a satisfied voice. "No wonder Bell was so nervous!"

"Do you think Graham Crosby found out about them?" wondered Newton aloud as they drove back to Ipswich. "If they have them there, what's the betting that they have them at the other shop and garage?"

"I think you are going to have a busy Saturday applying for warrants", grinned Webb. Seeing as they have a car wash operated by foreigners, why don't we get some immigration chaps and customs and excise in on it as well? Even if they are legitimate, it may shake them into telling the truth."

In fact, that wasn't the only thing to deal with when the pair returned to the office on Saturday morning.

Chapter 7. Saturday 10th October, Ipswich

It seemed as if everyone had something to show to Webb and Newton when they entered the office on Saturday morning.

DC Gatesby had visited the health centre and found out that Graham Crosby had been treated with anti-depressants when his Grandmother died but turned down the opportunity to see a counsellor. He wasn't currently being treated for anything and was not on any repeat medication. They also confirmed his home address.

Catchpole and Winter had visited it, and the key initially found on the body opened it. The house had not been broken into, and there was the usual junk mail accumulating on the doormat. There were a few one-person microwave meals in the freezer and the typical contents in the fridge and cupboard for a young person living alone, such as small size packs, pot noodles, tinned beans and biscuits. There was a landline phone socket with no telephone plugged into it. Crosby only used it for the internet, it appeared. They had brought back a laptop computer, spare door keys and some papers, but nothing extraordinary, it seemed. They would go through it all today.

They had taken the opportunity to question the next-door neighbours. One hardly knew him as they had moved in only recently. However, Mrs

Gilson was a fount of information, and DC Winter read straight from his notebook her verbatim comments:

"I knew Mrs Crosby for more than 15 years, a lovely lady. Her daughter was a single mother, and when she died from cancer, she took in her son Graham and brought him up as her own. He was about eleven at the time, I think – he was certainly at senior school by then. She brought him up very well, how to say 'please' and 'thank you' and be polite. He did well at school, and she supported him to go to university, although she told me that she missed him. He used to come home in the holidays. I thought university might make him a bit more outgoing, but he still seemed quite reserved. Anyway, she died of old age, and he came back very upset. I saw him at the funeral, and then he must have gone back to Cambridge. Mrs Crosby was very proud of him and told me that she would leave the house to him when she went so that he would always have a home. I haven't seen too much of him since he came back here, but he always smiles and says, "Hello Mrs Gilson", if he spots me."

"If we cannot find any close relatives, we may need that Mrs Gilson to identify the body formally", commented Webb. "She knows him. Maybe you can handle that DC Winter please, as you have already made a connection with her?"

Webb asked Newton to brief them all on their visit to the petrol station yesterday and told them to expect to be going on simultaneous raids on Monday morning with customs and immigration staff at the three linked businesses.

The next job was to analyse the mobile phone contents, but Colin Newton raised a suspicion. "Isn't it a bit odd that the same person who helped find the body is also the one who also helpfully 'finds' the phone and wallet?" he asked.

"I don't like coincidences", declared Webb. " See what you can find out about him – I will handle getting the warrants and liaising with the other agencies. The rest of you go through the phone and laptop thoroughly. Identify any contacts or numbers in it, social media, pictures, whatever you can find – check it out between you. If you get any problems with access or passwords, call up forensics: That young fellow Gideon with the beard is a whiz, although I don't know if he is on duty today."

Newton scanned through the CCTV film he had collected from the garage yesterday, careful not to handle it with his fingers. He would get forensics to take Bells prints off it later. Sure enough, Graham Crosby could be seen crossing the forecourt at 6:02 pm. Several pedestrian customers visited between then and 7:00 pm, and Bell could be seen leaving in a silver Nissan car about ten minutes later, having locked the door behind him. It was as Bell had told them last night. Nevertheless, he still took the film over to forensics to extract prints of Bell and anyone else who had handled it.

Being a Saturday in Dinsbourne, there were fewer dog walkers on the field. Gilly had tried to avoid working as a dog walker at weekends when she started up her small business and succeeded. People who wanted their dogs walked whilst at work tended to be home at weekends to do it themselves. Norma Livingstone walked Bella later in the day. If the weather were fine, she would leave her children on the swings while she exercised him. Her husband had to work nearly every weekend when the DIY Warehouse was at its busiest. Stan and Louise tended to get up later at the weekend, and despite their best intentions, they sometimes didn't walk James. He wasn't that enthusiastic either.

Sandra Gray found just Jim and John there when she followed her usual routine. She knew that Veronica sometimes went further afield out into the country at weekends. Jim said that he was actually on his way home, having worked through the night with Rex at his side. "If he has a trot around and breakfasts with me when I get home, maybe he'll let me get some sleep!" he suggested.

"Jimbo wakes me up when he thinks it's time to get up in the morning. He sleeps on the bed with me. I think maybe Rex and Fi are a bit too big for that," laughed Sandra.

"Too right", replied John. I tried to get Fi to sleep downstairs when we first got her as a rescue, but I think she must have been used to sleeping beside the bed. She howled until we let her up, and what's worse is that she snores and takes up the rest of the bedroom."

"Rex sleeps beside the bed as well", added Jim. "He always has done, and he is company if I wake up in the night. I have bad dreams sometimes," he said.

"Try a drop of two of lavender oil on your pillow", advised Sandra. "Somebody recommended it to me after my Bill died, and it's safer than taking tablets," Jim said that it sounded a good idea, but privately thought that he would never completely get rid of Bosnia's nightmare visions, whatever he did.

Back at the police squad room, it was found that Graham Crosby had not been an enthusiast for cyber-security and still had the factory preset of 0000 as the password for both the mobile phone and computer. He had been on a Facebook group at university, but the posts were mainly students seeking help with their work and occasionally invites to parties. He had stopped posting to it the previous April. He was still in an England Rugby Fans group but didn't seem to post to it much.

The website history and saved favourites were mainly due to his academic interests, although he sometimes looked at eBay and Amazon. More recently, there were some views of a relatively tame free porn site that were not thought to be unusual for a young man without a girlfriend.

His ex-girlfriend Madeline did feature heavily in his email history: love notes that Peggy categorised as 'innocently sweet', arrangements for dates but more latterly pleas to get back in touch and return his phone calls. "Listen to this one," said Gilly;

Dearest Madeline, RU OK? I worry about you because I cannot get an answer. How about I take out a punt on the River Cam? We could have a picnic, and you could wear that big straw hat that makes you look even lovelier than usual. Or we could do something else if you prefer. I just want to see you again and talk. Have I done something wrong? If I have, I am sorry, but please speak to me about it. I couldn't get to you by phone. Have you run out of funds for it? You don't seem to be coming to lectures either. Old Scoresby was a hoot the other day talking about some of the Bosnian Serbs' private lives. Love Graham xxx

"He sounds very 'loved up' if a bit pathetic," judged Peggy. "Quite romantic!" Her male colleagues grunted in mutual derision.

"Well, between the girly porn and the emails, I guess we can rule out him being gay or bisexual", commented Will. "It eliminates the need to check out whether it could have been a fall out between Crosby and another gay male", he added.

The emails were methodically stored in a set of folders: 'Madeline', 'Grandma' (including details of the will, funeral, house transfer etc.) 'House' included utility bills and contracts, solicitor letters and 'Uni' was for his studies, including emails between him and his tutor, which confirmed the reasons for him 'dropping out.'

The document files were all to do with his studies, and some were in Polish and French. None were dated for after the time he had left university.

There were a couple of 'shoot them up' computer games that he seemed to play quite regularly and a music player from a streaming site. "He seems to have a penchant for sad love songs and indie rockers", commented Winter.

"I would have been suspicious if we'd found that he loved Gangsta Rap", responded Will Gatesby, chuckling. "Not the type, it seems. You can tell a lot about a person from their music and book choices," he continued. "I wouldn't have been surprised if he had been into Classical music. I'm into hard house, drums and bass stuff," he added.

"I picked some you lot at that rave with a load of ecstasy outside Felixstowe last year", joked Peggy. "Have you got the Acid Smiley teeshirt?" she teased. Gatesby ignored her, refusing to be pulled in by the bait. Trying to deflect attention, he countered with, "what are you into then? Country and Western?"

"What an insult!" Peggy retaliated. "I'm a solid Bruce Springsteen fan. Plus a bit of local boy Ed Sheeran, of course. What about you, Chris? Are you a closet Death Metal man?"

"Hardly – more Coldplay and Maroon 5, I'd guess", replied Chris. "Anyway, hadn't we better try and find out what else is on this laptop?"

Getting back to work, they found a Pictures folder. It only contained a couple of dozen shots, appearing to have been taken on a mobile phone. Most of them were of Madeline at different places plus some of the other students at a party, dated the previous December. None of them was taken after he departed from Cambridge. They passed the machine on to forensics to search for any useful hidden or deleted files.

Disappointed with the results from the laptop, attention was focused on the mobile phone. He had used it for emails as well, but these had already been examined. There were some recent text messages between himself and Norman Bell at the garage. They all seemed to be making arrangements for shifts such as 'Can you cover Wednesday?' and brief 'Yes' and 'No' answers, occasionally illustrated with a smiley emoticon. Further back, there were text messages between him and Madeline. "Not the king of sexting' was the comment from Chris, which made his colleagues wonder what was hidden on his private phone. Nobody knew whether Chris had a current girlfriend, and he was coy about his love life.

Graham had very few contact numbers stored in his mobile, and they were quickly identified: Madeline, Grandma, Petrol Station, Tutor and Doctor. It seemed an insubstantially small list for a young man. It increased the likelihood that comments about him being 'quiet' and 'sad' were accurate.

All of the photos on his laptop were also duplicated upon the phone, indicating that they had been taken on the phone and downloaded. However, after a gap in dates since leaving uni, two new ones were taken on Saturday 3rd October 2020 at 3:35 pm. They had not yet been transferred to the laptop.

DS Colin Newton ignored the banter of his colleagues in the side room. He relished the task of investigating the background to Jim Coxall. He prided himself on being quite nifty at getting information through IT methods. The most prominent place to look was in the PNC - Police National Criminal records database and HOLMES 2.

Disappointingly there was not so much as a speeding ticket for Coxall. Next, he simply put his name into a search engine. Several matches came up for 'Jim Coxall', but only one matched the approximate age, nationality and location criteria.

It was a news story from a local newspaper about Coxall saying that he had served in the Royal Military Police in Northern Ireland and the Balkans. There was a picture of him in uniform crouched with his dog. The article said that he had been saved by his service dog Rex from being seriously injured by a booby trap bomb in Bosnia. The story went onto say how his unit was on a mission to arrest someone from a building in Sarajevo; when they got there, Rex had growled and blocked Jim from going inside. It was so unlike him to disobey that Jim became suspicious and lobbed a brick through the open doorway. The entire building was demolished in the ensuing booby trap explosion, and Jim and his mates survived unharmed.

"He doesn't sound like an archetypal villain, serving in the Military Police," said Newton to Chris, who had come over to offer him a cup of tea.

Chris looked at the screen over his shoulder and commented, "That may explain why he was keen to take command of the dog walkers and be observant enough to help us. Once a policeman, always a policeman, my Dad used to say."

"You could have a point there", admitted Newton. However, when Chris had gone to make everyone tea, he gave one more check to Coxall's statement. The interviewing constable had asked everyone their occupation, and Coxall had responded, "Security Guard." Could there be something in his work that may bring him into conflict with Graham Crosby? Was Coxall involved in the smuggling operation to get illicit tobacco into the UK? Having been in the Army, he may well have had the opportunity to make contacts with foreign criminals, especially being in the Military Police. He googled 'Balkans + crime.'

There were many pages of results, so he chose to look at one with more reliable credentials: The Times newspaper. It appeared that one of their top illegal exports were sub-standard cigarettes that did not comply with health standards in the EC. 'Wouldn't want them to make unhealthy fags', he thought sarcastically. 'Ours are so much better at killing you!' He hated smoking. His earlier suspicions seem to be on far safer ground now. However, the following paragraph caught his eye as well.

It dealt with the number of war crimes by all sides still not adequately investigated and said that many suspected war criminals were hiding in sympathetic communities. Could Coxall have been involved in investigating in his role there? It was then that something hit him: what was Graham Crosby's area of studies? The Balkan Conflict and Modern Languages, which included Polish! Had Crosby found more than was safe for him? He could read Polish and French documents that had not been translated into English, possibly including ones alleging wartime atrocities for all the region's parties, including the British Army.

At that point, Chris brought the teas back into the room for the team, interrupting his chain of thought. Handing Newton his, he said, "come and view what we found on Crosby's phone, and see what you make of it."

Chris moved over to the other group of desks, and Gatesby gave up his seat so that Chris could see the computer screen. "Look, these two pictures that were taken on the Saturday before he died. It's a group of lads at a carwash, presumably the one at the garage."

Just then, DCI Webb returned from obtaining search warrants for all three premises. "The magistrate did not take kindly to being disturbed on a Saturday", he grumbled. DS Newton invited him to view the pictures with him and brought him up to date on what they had been finding out.

"Yes, it looks like the carwash at Main Road Petrol Station", confirmed Newton. "One wonders why it should be of interest to him? They don't seem aware that they are being photographed. It seems to have been taken through the shop window at the side – you can see the newspapers and magazines in the corner of the picture. They are just inside the door to the right. Hang on! Don't a lot of those carwash operations employ foreigners? They come over from places like Latvia and Poland, don't they?"

"That's right", chipped in Peggy. "I use one in Ipswich for my car. They do it a lot more thoroughly than them old carwash machines as well, inside and out. I wouldn't fancy their job, though, soaking wet and out in all types of weather. They cannot be paid a lot, which is probably why you rarely see any local lads working at it."

"Yes, but hang on!" exclaimed Newton. "Graham Crosby studied the Balkans at university and foreign languages. Some of his language course was in Polish, which I suppose helped him to read stuff directly without it having to be translated."

"That is a good point", encouraged Webb.

"Then that could also be a possible connection between him and a soldier that served out there, such as Jim Coxall", continued Newton. "The article I found said about the Balkans, which was mainly Bosnia and Croatia, but I think Poland, Latvia and Lithuania were involved as well", reasoned Newton. "Alternatively, it may mean that Crosby could talk to the car wash workers in their language! That might have been dangerous if he found out that they were illegal immigrants or even used in what they call 'modern slavery.' I learnt about it on that safeguarding course I attended, and it isn't just textile factories, sex workers and maids. They have found some people being forced to work for nothing on carwashes to repay being smuggled over here."

"It's a horrible business", agreed Webb. "All the more reason to get Immigration and Trading Standards involved. We need to hit all three places together so they don't tip each other off. It's no good going in too early: I doubt that the car wash will start up until 8 am, so best not to hit them until 8:45 am. Three sites are going to spread us a bit thin. DS Newton and DC Winter will go to Main Road Petrol Station, myself to the other petrol station at Harvest Way.

DC Catchpole and DC Gatesby, you hit the MiniMarket on The Square. I don't think you will need Immigration there, but you will need to facilitate the Trading Standards search. I will talk to 'His Lordship' about getting some uniforms to back up each operation. If we find any dodgy tobacco, then Trading Standards will want to examine the houses and cars of the owner Colin Burwell and the managers of the two petrol stations. Keep a lookout for any keys that don't seem to 'belong.' They may have a lock-up garage or something to store the main bulk of shipments. Make sure you know all the details for each site and select a place nearby to meet up with the other agencies beforehand."

With that, Webb headed upstairs with enough reasons to justify what he wanted in resources. Later he had several telephone conversations with staff from Customs and Excise, Trading Standards and Immigration. He persuaded them this was a golden opportunity for them all.

Just then, an email from forensics told Newton that prints from the film case had been taken and identified as belonging to Norman Bell, who had a police record. He looked it up: There was nothing recent on there, but he had been found guilty of Actual Bodily Harm in his teens when he had got into a fight at a pub. He had broken the nose and teeth of another customer. At twenty-two years old, he was convicted of receiving stolen property, namely a stereo system from a burglar who sold it to him.

There was nothing on his record since then, but that didn't mean he had led a blameless life since, just that he hadn't been caught. Interestingly the business owner Colin Burwell was linked to his file as a brother-in-law. That may explain why he was willing to employ someone with a minor criminal record as a manager, thought Newton.

Burwell himself had been convicted of selling alcohol from his shop to a minor two years ago but was otherwise free of convictions. Newton printed out these records for the officers conducting raids and updated the whiteboard. With the other information that the others had obtained today, it was getting crowded with a lot more detail.

DCI Webb emerged from his office looking pleased and told them all that the raids were definitely on. They would each get back up of at least one extra uniformed constable, and the other agencies were just waiting for them to email them the time and rendezvous points for Monday morning. "Get a good days rest tomorrow. You will be very busy on Monday, and I want you all at your best. Good hunting!" Webb exhorted.

After finishing up their notes and liaising with the other agencies, the rest of the team all departed for the night in good spirits, but Newton had returned to his enquiry into Jim Coxall. He put through a request for a copy of his Army records and mobile phone log before retiring for the night.

On Sunday, Webb took the opportunity to indulge in his one vice: the care of his precious roses. It was time to deadhead and prune the late bloomers, and he had spent a pleasant two hours in the garden before his wife Alice called him in for dinner. She had long ago accepted her third place behind police work and roses in her husband's priorities.

Inevitably Colin Newton exerted himself sweatily for a couple of hours at the gym and relaxed in the café afterwards, trying to chat to a decidedly uninterested lady that had caught his eye. Peggy Catchpole studied police procedures for her upcoming exams whilst her husband was on duty. It wasn't the best way to relax, but she was determined to make at least Detective Sergeant. After that, she would just see where her ambitions took her.

Will Gatesby was the best at relaxing: he split his day between a trip down to a local wood with his binoculars for a spot of birdwatching, a pint in the local pub and then settled down in an armchair to read the autobiography of an explorer. He dozed off after a couple of chapters.

Chris Winter found it quite hard to switch off from the job. He arranged to take his new girlfriend Sara out for a pub lunch but found it hard to focus on some of what she was talking about. Tales of the 'spiteful bitch' who controlled her office wasn't as riveting as the theories he had going through his head about the murder case. What was worse was he couldn't share any information with her because she was a civilian. No wonder people like Peggy Catchpole married another police officer! The lunch ended on a sour note when he gave Sara an inappropriate response when he couldn't concentrate on what she was saying. She sat in stony silence on the car journey back and didn't try to arrange another date as she had done before. It did not bode well for the future.

Chapter 8. Morning of Monday 12th October, Dinbourne.

DC Catchpole sat at her Renault's wheel in a town centre carpark just up the road from the MiniMarket on The Square. DC Gatesby was in the passenger seat, and a uniformed PC Wicks crammed onto the back seat. It was 8:30 am, and they knew that they had over ten minutes to wait before they may move off. The guys from Trading Standards were in a small white van beside them. The gruff voice of DCI Webb crackled over the radio: "All in position? over."

"DC Gatesby here. In position with our 'friends'. Over." They heard a similar message from DS Newton. The ten minutes dragged, and Gatesby fidgeted with his hands. Catchpole frequently checked her watch and rubbed the condensation off the screen, and the PC shifted his position to try to get his long legs comfortable in the restricted back seat space. Finally, it was time, and DC Gatesby gave a thumbs-up to the van as they moved off. The two motors pulled up right outside the shop, ignoring the double yellow lines with a card left in the dash that said 'Police on call.'

Colin Burwell was behind the till by the door as they entered, and looked visibly shocked at the police warrants and uniform. "I understand that you may have supplies of tobacco for which tax duty has not been paid. We have warrants to search these premises, your home and other businesses. Would you like to show us where they are, sir?" asked DC Catchpole.

Without any resistance, Burwell pointed to a cardboard box beneath the till. The pair from Trading Standards moved forward and picked it up. Looking inside, they nodded. The PC moved to the door, changed the sign to 'Closed', and clicked the lock whilst DC Gatesby approached Mrs Burwell, who had been standing transfixed by the shelf she was refilling. He indicated that she should join the others and went out back to the storeroom and found their son Nigel oblivious to what was happening. He was asked to join his parents. They were all told that they were being arrested for "selling or distributing counterfeit goods, supplying tobacco without a combined health warning and supplying tobacco without a general health warning" and given an official caution.

The three were left in the PC's hands whilst Trading Standards searched the storeroom for further supplies. Spotting a large cardboard box on top of a freezer was a lucky early find. As the Trading Standards officers continued checking unsuccessfully for fake alcohol and perfume brands, the two detectives were bundling up a laptop and every bit of paper they could find in the office into large evidence bags, which they sealed. With the contents of a filing cabinet, it amounted to half a dozen large sacks.

DC Gatesby got on the radio to DCI Webb: "We have a positive result here, sir. I'm going to call up a waggon to take three family members to the station, then continue to the home. Over." He persuaded Colin Burwell to lend them a key to his house rather than break in and cause damage.

"Well done, everybody. I will see you there with the manager from here. Make sure they don't get a chance to talk to each other, over" responded Webb.

After the family had gone off in a police van with the constable, the Trading Standards guys found a key to the garage at Burwell's home. It was half full of cigarettes and tobacco. "This is the best find in a long time," they said. "Nice one!" The detectives found another laptop and papers, which they bagged up and took to the police station.

Meanwhile, DCI Webb was having similar success at the other petrol station. The manager Alan Bowry, who openly had little liking for the owner, admitted that he had been told to sell the cigarettes when the other staff were not present. He showed them a large carton labelled for breakfast cereal on a high storeroom shelf with the goods inside. He was arrested but said he never stored them himself – they were delivered directly to the store by Colin Burwell. The Trading Standards officers said that they would go around and check. The manager said that his wife would be at home with their baby. Over at the carwash, some stern-looking immigration officers had arrested the four workers and were taking them to their home to look for passports, as none could prove who they were. They all seemed very frightened, and one was in tears.

It was a similar situation at the Main Road carwash, with the four workers there arrested. A customer was most irate because his car was left covered in suds and threatened to call the police. An Immigration Officer intervened: "That will be next door, sir then – they are in there, but I think they are a bit busy at the moment. You haven't paid yet, so why don't you get that hose and rinse it off yourself? It will be a cheap visit!"

As DS Newton entered the shop with the PC and two Trading Standards staff, Carl, the spotty youth, was on the till again. Bell was in the back office and saw a police uniform and the detective he recognised on the CCTV monitor and some commotion around the carwash. He panicked and left by the backdoor. Outside, his car was blocked in by Webb's car and the other ones from Trading Standards and Immigration. Swearing to himself, he had to walk around to the front. He was already crossing the road when Newton glanced out of the window as he made his way to the storeroom. Spotting Burwell racing off, he swiftly headed for the front door, but his path was blocked by an old lady choosing sweets. He called out to the Constable to join him.

Although he wasn't particularly fit, Bell ran as fast as he could. He had a considerable lead on his pursuers by now and headed down Church Road, thinking that he may be able to lose them by ducking into a shop. However, he was still in sight of Newton, although separated by a considerable distance. With the benefit of his fitness routine, Newton was gaining on him. The uniformed officer was winded and flagging and stopped to radio in for back up.

Glancing back and seeing his pursuers, Bell realised that he would be seen and trapped by going into a shop to hide. He continued through the Recreation Ground gate. As he approached the gate, Newton could see the bunch of dog walkers distributed around the field. "Stop him!" he screamed at the top of his voice. "Police! Stop!" Jim Coxall looked up and took in the situation, including a policeman in uniform in the distance. Bending, he unclipped the lead and slipped the muzzle off his dog and pointed at the fugitive. "Rex! Seize him!" he commanded. Overjoyed at being back in working mode after so long retired, the dog travelled towards Bell as fast as juicy gossip.

The other dog walkers had already dispersed from their usual morning chat, so they were spread around the field. As usual, Gilly Wallis was preparing to leave by the Talbot Road gate with her four minuscule pooches but heard the shouts. The little dogs would be more likely injured if she tried to use them against this big man hurtling towards her, but there was a straightforward, safe thing that she could do: showing great presence of mind, she slammed the gate closed from the outside and tied it up using her multiple dog leads. Panting, she peered through the mesh as the situation unfolded.

Caught up in the general excitement but not understanding what was going on, Jimbo the Jack Russell chased after Rex, followed by Sandra. Not wanting to be left out or upstaged by Jim, John Westrup released Fi the Irish Wolfhound. True to form and daftness, she ran in the opposite direction, woofing and wagging her tail enthusiastically. Norma Livingstone put her dog, Bella, back on her lead. Her husband would give her hell if he found out that she had got involved. James the Labrador wagged his tail and toddled ponderously across the field towards the action, followed by Stan and Louise. She was already on her phone to the police, saying that "something is happening, but I'm not sure what."

Inevitably the pair of springer spaniels Pat and Billy thought it was all a great game and ran around barking and wagging their tails with exuberance and general ability to get in everybody's way. This included Norman Bell, who had to swerve to try and avoid them. There was no escape from a dog as fast as a focused Doberman. Bell raised his arm protectively as Rex sprung to have it firmly locked onto by a very firm pair of jaws that pushed it and Bell to the ground. "Help! Get him off me! he screamed, terrified. Rex dribbled on his sleeve, looked him in the eyes and gave a low, threatening growl. "Good boy Rex!" gasped Jim catching up. "Hold!"

"Good boy indeed", congratulated DS Newton, also now catching up to the panicking figure prostrate on the ground. Grinning, he added quietly, "I really must ask you to get your dog to release him, but maybe you could just wait until I have located my handcuffs, please." He eyed Rex nervously and kept his distance from him.

"I'm in no hurry", replied Jim smiling. "I'm Jim Coxall, and we are both ex-Royal Military Police. Rex is completely under control." Bell looked up wide-eyed and did not seem terribly convinced of this. The dog that still held his arm in its slavering jaws was continuing to give a rumbling, low warning growl. Wisely, he stopped struggling.

"Ah, Mr Coxall, you were the guy who found the wallet and phone. Thanks very much for that," said Newton, recognising to whom he was talking from the newspaper picture. Jim had not changed much since it was taken.

Suddenly, the field was full of police officers, alerted by the Constable's radio and spurred on by Louise's phone call. They entered through gates at both ends of the field. Gilly had untied her entrance when she saw them arrive. The rest of the dog walkers had also gathered around when Bell was cautioned and led away in handcuffs. Another officer collected Carl, the assistant at the petrol station. He claimed not to know anything about foreign cigarettes that Trading Standards found beneath the counter and in the warehouse. After a statement was taken at the police station, he was released, as there was no evidence to the contrary. The police and the dog walkers praised Rex and his master. He explained that this was the sort of thing they had been trained for in the Royal Miltary Police. The dog wouldn't obey anyone except Jim, so as Rex was close to retirement age, they let him keep his furry friend when he finished his service at the end of 2013.

"That sounds interesting", purred Gill. "You must tell me more about it some time" before she had to leave to return the four little dogs to their owners. Sandra quietly observed and smiled to herself. Veronica added, "I hope that was the murderer they just caught. We can all rest easier then."

"I recognise him from the petrol station," said Stan.

"Is that so?" asked John, who had finally managed to retrieve Fi back onto her lead. "Do you know his name?"

"Oh yes, it was Norman Bell", answered Louise triumphantly. "He and his wife and child were registered at the Medical Centre, where I used to work."

John walked away, his mobile phone already in his hand to pass on the news to his old colleagues.

Chapter 9. The afternoon of Monday 12th October, Ipswich

The interview by Catchpole and Gatesby with Alan Bowry was reasonably straightforward. He admitted to getting a cash bonus for selling illegal cigarettes and had been instructed to do it when other staff were not present. The money did not go through the till. It was kept in a big envelope that was handed to Colin Burwell when he delivered more. He said that he knew nothing about the carwash operation. He understood that they were a separate business that rented Burwell's space, who gave them a water supply and permission to use the area at the end of the forecourt. He was charged and released on bail.

They watched through a one-way mirror whilst DCI Webb interviewed Colin Burwell. Having already admitted his involvement, he tried to blame Norman Bell as much as possible and say that his wife and son were not involved. Webb did not believe the latter and later charged them as accessories to the crimes.

"I employed Norman Bell because he was married to my sister and out of work," said Burwell. "At the time, the car wash machines were both broken and very expensive to mend. They are still in pieces from when I tried to repair them myself. They have always been unreliable, so when Norman suggested that he could get the space rented out to a manual car wash company, I agreed. It made good business sense: an income from the area was better than the old broken machines, plus increased traffic for petrol and shop. It is tough to compete with the out of town hypermarkets and oil company garages, you know," he continued. "Most of the price of the fuel goes in tax to the government, and we still have to try to get near the lower prices elsewhere."

"You will have me in tears soon, but do go on", commented Webb.

"Once he had those going, it was difficult to back out," Burwell said. "I sensed there was something 'dodgy' about the car washes, but they were separate companies, and they always paid their bills on time."

"So when did you start buying iffy tobacco then," asked Webb, eager to keep him talking. He could get hold of the finer details later.

"About six months ago, he came to me with a plan: continue selling some proper fags to seem above board, but for the managers to supply cut-price stock from abroad to known regular customers. Word quickly spread, and soon we had a regular clientele. I thought it was getting out of control, but he told me we couldn't back out: the suppliers were hard men and likely to get at our families if they thought we had become a risk. It is not just my wife and son – he is married to my sister. I do not believe he treated her right, but she stayed because of the baby. A fortnight ago, she fled, and he doesn't know where. I do – she is safe with a friend up North. I had become terrified of him myself – he has been violent in the past, you know."

"Yes, I do know", confirmed Webb, but it was you that dealt with Graham Crosby, wasn't it?"

"No! That is a lie. I didn't know anything about this chap Crosby. Norman had employed him as a casual: he said that it was more flexible and kept them on their toes to keep the job. The first I knew about it was when Norman told me on the phone that he hadn't shown up for work or called in, so he would be covering his shift until he could get someone else."

"Well, I only have your word for that, don't I" growled Webb. "We will be keeping you here until I have had a word with him. I should think about getting yourself a lawyer," he added and indicated to the PC standing by that he could return him to the holding cells.

By the time that Webb exited the interview, Newton had returned. They went up into Webb's office to exchange information and decide tactics on interviewing Bell. Newton told him what had been going on, and asked "You don't believe that Burwell made the killing do you, sir? He doesn't appear to have the guts, whilst Bell has form for violence."

"Oh no", replied Webb. "I just wanted to frighten him into spilling as much on Bell as possible. It seems it was only the petrol station managers selling the tobacco. They didn't trust the assistants with it."

"I wouldn't be surprised if he stays clammed up", commented Newton. "He has already asked for a duty lawyer" and appears to be a hardened individual."

"Yes, you are probably right, DCI Newton, but that doesn't mean we cannot try, does it? Especially if we don't play all our cards at once. Let's see how loyal he is to Burwell if he thinks he has already dropped him in it."

"There is one piece of evidence that I rushed to the lab, sir. We cannot legitimately use it until it has been tested, but that may be to our advantage. I think it would be good to delay seeing him as long as possible to give forensics a chance."

"Well, I wanted him to sit and stew for a bit to soften him up," said Webb. "I wonder if the canteen has a suitable salad for you to partake of today? I shall be going for the pork chops and apple crumble myself."

"You know, I may even join you in that. I think I burned enough calories this morning chasing Bell down that road," said Newton with a grin.

After a leisurely lunch, the pair joined Bell and his lawyer in an interview room. The evidence recorder was switched on, and Bell was reminded he was under caution. The lawyer stated that his client declined to answer any of their questions.

"That is his legal right, but he wouldn't be helping himself," said Webb ", since his boss Colin Burwell has already stitched him up and given us a confession. Now, Mr Bell, do you admit to arranging shipments of illegal tobacco and cigarettes and selling them?"

"No comment," said a stony-faced Norman Bell.

"Do you admit to contracting with a hand car wash company, knowing that they had illegal immigrants working for them?"

"No comment."

Webb continued to ask questions about the tobacco and car wash but deliberately avoided mentioning Graham Crosby. Occasionally Newton would add further comments or word the questions differently, but the response was always 'no comment.' Behind the cover of the desk, Webb pointed to his watch, and Newton gave a brief nod and looked towards the door.

"I protest!" interrupted the Duty Solicitor indignantly at last. "I clearly stated that my client declined to answer any questions. You are now repeating yourself to the extent that it could be construed as harassment and inappropriate behaviour. I must insist that you …" His words were interrupted by a sharp knock on the door and without waiting for a response an entry.

"For the benefit of the recording, DC Catchpole has entered and handed me a note." He paused, read it and passed it to Newson, who gave a slight smirk. "Thank you, DC Catchpole. For the benefit of the recording, she has now left the room." Webb nodded to Newton.

Newton knew that Bell must be wondering what was in the note, as must his solicitor. He deliberately paused and leant back in his chair as if he had all the time in the world for them to consider that. Then he broke the suspense and spoke very slowly and deliberately, with his eyes fixed on those of Bell.

"Earlier today, after you had been apprehended from guiltily running away and transported here, I carried on with the two gentlemen from Trading Standards to your home. We had a warrant to inspect it for evidence of a crime. You will undoubtedly be relieved that we did not find any more of those illegal cigarettes since they were all at Colin Burwell's home. We did remove some papers, which will be returned to you when we have finished looking at them very carefully." He paused to let this sink in. Bell seemed to relax a little from the tense state he had been experiencing. He knew that they were unlikely to have found anything but money.

"We found a carrier bag in your wardrobe stuffed with money. This note says that your prints are all over it." Bell shrugged his shoulders and rolled his eyes. The detectives had decided to wait until it had been fingerprinted and counted before bringing that in as additional evidence. It contained several thousand pounds. "Would you like to explain how it got there?" asked Newton, raising his eyebrows.

"No comment," continued Bell, looking straight ahead.

"Imagine our surprise when we checked the garden shed for contraband before we left", Newton continued. "It was locked, so we had to break the hasp off. It fell on the ground, and as I did not want to leave any more mess than necessary, being a diligent police officer, I bent down to pick it up. What did I see but something shoved underneath the raised floor of the shed? The length of pipe with which you murdered Graham Crosby, some tissues and your sweatshirt with some blood on it!" he boomed, getting right into Bell's face. "That note just confirmed that the blood is Cosby's, and the prints left on the tissues and pipe are yours! The

142

serial number on the pipe identifies it as a component of a particular automatic carwash machine. No doubt it will match the one at Main Road Garage!"

Bell looked stunned, and he started sweating and shaking. "No, you can't pin this on me! he yelled, standing up from the chair.

"Sit down, Bell!" barked Webb, and the solicitor encouraged him to do so. "Norman Bell, I am charging you with the murder of Graham Cosby on or about Monday 5th October. You will be remanded in custody while further investigations are made. Further charges are likely to follow."

After a few private words with the solicitor, Bell was led back to a cell. Webb and Newton grinned at each other, and Webb said, "The thrill of getting the bastard never goes away. My advice to you is 'if you ever lose that thrill, give up, son.' They ascended the stairs to the office, where Webb put on a mock scowl at the team expectedly awaiting them. "Haven't you lot got reports to write up?" he bellowed. Then he grinned. "Well, leave them until tomorrow – the first drink is on me!"

The impromptu party at a local pub lasted for a lot longer than one drink. "A great team job," said Webb as he complimented the squad. He also took time to speak to every individual member and praised their efforts before exiting to let them let their collective hair down without him being present. He was happy to go home to the long-suffering Alice and put his feet up with a re-heated dinner and an old Ealing comedy film on the television.

Chapter 10. Tuesday 13th October, Dinbourne

Inevitably there was a lot of excited chatter on the Recreation Ground on Tuesday morning. Everyone gathered around Rex and patted him and told him what a good dog he was again. The story had made the regional tv news, and one national newspaper had picked up on it. Jim modestly spread praise around the others. "Did you see Gilly whip that gate shut sharply and tie it? That was quick thinking, Gilly! Our lovely Pat and Billy as well, they did a fine job of getting in his way Veronica!"

"They are very skilled at it", laughed Veronica. "As you all know, they practice getting in the way of everyone they meet every day!"

Stan and Louise arrived, and James waddled his way around the group wagging his tail. He wasn't sure why everybody was excited, but he liked happy people. It often meant that they gave him treats.

Norma stood chatting to Sandra as their dogs re-acquainted themselves. "Gilly is looking a lot happier today, don't you think?" asked Norma.

"Watch the looks that pass between her and Jim, and it may explain it", whispered Sandra confidentially.

"Really?" asked Norma.

"Trust me," said Sandra, pleased to share her secret. "Now that I have heard the victim's name and address on the news, I realised why he looked familiar on the front of the newspaper last week: he lived further up Talbot Road from me, on the other side. I did not know him, but I must have seen him walk past my home occasionally."

John Westrip tried to overhear what they were saying, from habit more than anything else but was unsuccessful. Fi looked up at him with a pair of deep, soulful eyes and gave his hand a gentle lick.

Jim wandered over to where Gilly had stopped to untangle her dogs once again. He asked her a question that had occurred to him at about three in the morning: "You clearly love dogs. Have you got one of your own?"

"Oh, yes," she replied. "A gorgeous Dalmation called Millie – I walk her later in the day.

"They are smashing dogs. I expect you'll know that they used to use them in a pair running alongside the gentries coaches. That's why they run so well, keeping up with the horses like that," continued Jim, gaining in confidence.

"No, I didn't know that. How interesting, and it explains a lot. Millie just loves to run but never has anyone to race around with her. I have to keep the clients dogs on the lead," explained Gilly.

"Maybe, if you don't mind, we could exercise them together sometime? I have to give him a run twice a day. I'm afraid that he turns his nose up at small dogs, though!" Gilly didn't say anything for a moment, thinking to herself. Jim looked a little worried that he had overstepped the mark with her. Taking pity on his expression and throwing caution to the winds, she replied, "OK, we could try it once! I will be at Spring Meadow Country Park this afternoon. Do you know it?"

"Yes, I do, just by the river. What time?" replied Jim eagerly.

"Let's say 2:30 pm. I will have picked up the other dogs from my customers by then."

"2:30 pm it is then," said Jim, beaming like a dolphin.

They did meet later that day, and Rex took to Millie immediately. They sped off in great circles around the meadow, chasing each other and then turning tail so that the chaser became the pursued. Gilly still had a Poodle and a Yorkie under her control, but they both laughed at their dog's exuberant play with happy grins as they walked together. "You never told me what Dobermans were bred for this morning," asked Gilly.

"A German tax collector bred them to protect him," said Jim.

"So does he do a good job of protecting you?"

"Very much so. Rex is very loyal, and he saved my life once." Jim went on to tell her the story, the first time he had done so to anyone in several years. "So yes, he does protect me from bad people, but not from a pretty face!" he finished.

Gilly had not been prepared for the compliment but received it with good grace. "You German tax collectors are all flatterers", she joked, "but I can see how you love your dog and how important he is to you."

"Yes, he is", admitted Jim, "and at the moment my only companion", he added.

"It is time to get my other dogs returned to their owners," said Gilly, avoiding for the moment the apparent implication of what Jim had just said. "Millie! Here girl!" Jim called Rex as well, and they praised their panting dogs when they returned. Jim also made a fuss of Millie, tickling her behind the ear, which she enjoyed. Gilly stroked Rex's head, who had come up to her for the first time since she had seen him a couple of months ago.

"You have got a friend there!" commented Jim. "He is very fussy who he associates with, like me. Thank you for this afternoon, for Rex and me," said Jim tentatively. "Would you like to do it again sometime?" he asked hopefully.

"Yes, I think I would like that, and I'm sure Millie would", replied Gilly. After they had parted, Jim walked back to his car with a decided spring in his step. Gilly left in a good mood as well. Jim seemed gentle, even shy despite his army background, and his rugged looks were handsome. She reached home, fed Millie and started to make an omelette for herself.

She looked down at her companion, sitting very near in the hope of a wayward scrap of cheese falling to the kitchen floor. "What do you think, Millie?" she asked. Millie wagged her tail, pleased to see her owner happy. "Maybe we will try to get to know him better", continued Gilly. "I guess that will mean him getting to know my story better as well, though," she thought doubtfully. "Well, he seemed honest with me, so I guess I owe him the same courtesy back, don't you reckon Millie? I can't imagine an ex-policeman going out at night to do burglaries." As she sat down with a tray on her lap to eat, she relaxed in front of her favourite teatime programme. "Was that a date?" she wondered. It was a long time since she had been dating, and she knew that it was a bit different nowadays, with texting and so on. Little did she know, but Jim was having those same thoughts at the same time.

Chapter 11. Tuesday 13th October, Ipswich.

Despite some members of the Murder Squad having bleary eyes and headaches, they were all present when DCI Webb entered the office. "Good Morning!" he greeted them, uncharacteristically cheerful. "Everything OK? No doubt you all have a lot of reports to catch up on, as do I. Any problems, ask DS Newton or me. We need to make sure that it is all faultless to make sure the court does them for everything. Cross the t's and dot the i's," he emphasised.

There was a renewed tapping of computer keys and squinting at notes handwritten in a hurry, occasionally interrupted by someone swearing to themselves or getting up to make tea. In his office, Webb was correlating the reports of Trading Standards from the various addresses. They confirmed that the cigarettes and tobacco were of substandard quality to UK regulations and had not had tax paid on them as well as ripping off trademarks from legitimate manufacturers. They were reporting directly to Her Majestys Revenue, and Customs (HMRC) and the eye-watering taxes and penalties they had calculated were enough to bankrupt the businesses. "Serves them right!" he muttered to himself.

The reports from the UK Immigration Service and Borders Agency were even more eye-opening. None of the six people working at the two carwashes was legally in the UK or had work visas. Therefore, the two Polish Dyzinski brothers who employed the other six were liable to a £10,000 fine for each of them, equalling £60,000. The Agency intended to go after the total amount by seizing cash, bank accounts, cars, houses or other property that belonged to them in lieu before deporting them to their countries of origin, either Poland, Lithuania or Ukraine. Charges against illegal imprisonment were also made, but they were unsure whether they would stick. They had also been onto authorities abroad, and the two brothers would be arrested for part of a people-trafficking operation on arrival. "Yes!" thought Webb, smacking his fist into the palm of the other hand since he had no direct evidence to get a conviction for it this side of the Channel. Crown Prosecution Service was unlikely to think it worthwhile pursuing.

The startling reports of how the workers had been treated were most disturbing: the house into which all six had been locked each night was unsafe electrically, and the only toilet was partly broken. Very little food was found, and apparently, they were mainly given bread and rice to survive on with some manky vegetables. Threats of physical violence by the Dyzinski brothers were frequent, as were threats against family members still living abroad if the workers disobeyed, tried to communicate with the public or run away.

All talk with carwash customers had to be with one of the brothers who kept all cash. They were told that they would be kept working until they had 'paid off' the fee for smuggling them into the UK in a lorry, amounting to thousands of pounds. They were also told that the UK Police would not listen to their stories but simply beat them up and send them home without any court appeal.

All six workers were classed as being subject to 'Modern Slavery' under the UK safeguarding legislation. They received no money and only had the clothes they were wearing. Their passports had been taken away from them but were recovered at the house. One individual had plimsolls that had been badly affected by the constant exposure to water and cleaning fluids so that the soles had to be surgically removed from the skin of his feet by medical staff after the arrest. Even with a lifetime of police service behind him, Webb was aghast that people could be treated like that.

It was believed that the brothers paid £2000 per month for each of the carwash sites in cash. Bell kept the Main Road site cash, and the other was passed on to Burwell. 'No doubt the taxman will be interested to see whether that went through the books,' thought Webb, 'although it would partly explain the cash from the bottom of Bell's wardrobe.'

Webb had just stepped out of his office to get some tea when 'His Lordship' appeared through the main door to congratulate the team on doing a good job. After he had said his piece, DS Newton approached him. "Thank you, sir, it was a great team effort, but I wonder if we can use it to take action on an email you sent out recently: the one about being seen to work with the community. That group of dog walkers turned out to be useful: they found the body and didn't mess up the site, found the wallet and phone and of course, they helped to catch the fugitive Bell. One of them also rang our hotline with a name suggestion for the deceased and called control to send reinforcements when she thought we were in trouble. Is there some way we could recognise all of that and get some good PR as well, sir?"

"Good point DS Newton! I'm glad that someone reads my emails! I shall study your reports and have a good discussion about them with the Corporate Communications Department and the Chief Constable. That is exactly the sort of initiative I was talking about! This year, the public has been worried enough by pop star paedophiles, jihadists, tasers, elections, and women Bishops. We need to refocus attention on our partnership with the local community." He departed, beaming a rarely witnessed smile.

"You'll go very far!" growled Webb quietly to Newton. "Attitude like that you should make Inspector at least!" Newton wasn't entirely sure whether this was a compliment or sarcasm, so he said nothing and smiled.

Privately, as he sat back in his office with his delayed cup of tea, Webb smiled to himself and reflected that with a bit more experience, Newton might well go further in the Suffolk Police Force. It did no harm to occasionally play the system to your advantage, so good luck to him. He was still a bit young and cocky, but he did work hard and show a bit of initiative sometimes, he thought grudgingly. At least he had risen through uniform and wasn't on one of those wretched 'Graduate Fast Track' schemes!

Newton was, of course, unaware of the thoughts of his boss. Like a terrier with a rat, he had returned to poke at all the available information about Jim Coxall. Just because Bell was in the frame for the murder and other crimes, it did not signify that Coxall was not involved. The Army records had arrived attached to a secure email.

Coxall had joined the Army in 1993 at the age of 18, finishing twenty years later in November 2013. Entries showed various training dates and postings to Bosnia, Northern Ireland and Kosovo. There were also UK postings at major UK military centres such as Catterick and Colchester. Although the record did not show much descriptive material, there were details of good conduct medals and no mentions of being formally disciplined. It confirmed that he had been in the right places to contact criminals in the Balkans or be involved in war crimes.

Checking back to his witness statement, he was surprised to see that Coxall had said 'no' when asked if he had an email address. Whilst it wasn't impossible, few people of his age managed to avoid the internet. He had given a mobile phone number, and if it was a new enough model, his phone might provide him with internet access. The phone log that had just arrived wasn't much help: mainly calls between him and his employers, the security company. One number appeared to be someone of the same surname in Birmingham, probably a relative, and a couple at present unidentified. He would need to inquire further to locate them, but there was no traffic of calls outside of the UK, which was significant. Identifying which mobile phone mast he was connecting with was pointless: his home, the Recreation Field and the garage were all covered by the same one. Notably, there were no calls between Coxall and the Dyzinski brothers, Burwell or Bell. Without getting hold of bank accounts, there was no suggestion of any involvement in the crimes. Newton wrote up his investigations and saw Webb to confirm that they didn't want to pursue that line of the inquiry any further at present.

"Bell didn't seem to recognise Coxall when he was standing over him with the dog", commented Newton. "If Coxall was involved in any of this, I doubt that he would have voluntarily got involved by releasing his dog. It would have been easier for him to walk away."

"Yes, I agree", confirmed Webb. "Bell could have identified him to divert attention and shift the blame from himself. The fact that he didn't seems to put Coxall in the clear as an ex-copper trying his best to help us. You can close the book on him."

"I hope they make some charges stick to them to those couple of Poles, though!" exclaimed Newton vehemently.

"Careful how you word things, or they'll be having you up for racism!" cautioned Webb. "I have to say that I would very much like to see the Dyzinski brothers in a British prison cell for what they have done before they get deported back to their national authorities. Take a look at these reports now that I have finished reading them.

Mind you, don't tar them all with the same brush. When I was at school, there were several Polish kids in my class. I had a mate called Alex Stankovich. My dad told me that there was a whole squadron of Polish Hurricane fighter pilots and crew based locally during World War 2.

Many of them didn't want to go back to be under Russian control after the war and stayed here and married local girls. Some of them changed their names to something more pronounceable and English sounding; it was their kids at my school."

"Yes, I think I heard of an Ipswich Polish Society formed long before they joined the European Community. They helped uniform with a case when I was there," added Newton. "I didn't know they flew in the Battle of Britain, though."

"Look out of my window here", invited Webb. Did you know that all this area was once an airfield?" he asked.

"I guessed it might be" responded, Newton. "There are a couple of buildings that look like old hangars over the other side of the field, and that perimeter road is concrete like they used to make them in World War 2. There are a lot of them around Suffolk, aren't there, being close to Europe?"

"It goes further back than that", explained Webb. "The Royal Flying Corps was based here in World War 1. I was reading a book about it the other time. Then they turned it into a place for experimental aircraft between the wars. Old Barnes-Wallis worked on a rotating gun turret here before going off to invent the bouncing bomb. First, the RAF, then the Americans had it as an airbase during the last war. Now it is that little industrial estate and us."

"You are a mine of information, sir!" said Newton, quite genuinely surprised. "Maybe I should try and get back to reading more books", he added.

"In this job, you never know when a little bit of information that you tucked away as useless comes in handy", instructed Webb. "As they say, information is power, and in this last case, we didn't have any until we could find out who the victim was."

"You're right there", confirmed Newton. "Well, I'd better go and finish up the file on Coxall to give some knowledge to someone else in the future," he said, excusing himself from the room. Webb's thoughtful gaze followed him out of the office as he reached for another humbug.

Chapter 12. Wednesday 14th October, Ipswich.

At about 10 am on Wednesday, Webb received word that Bell wanted to make a statement. He wasn't surprised as the solicitor would have probably told him that the evidence presented so far would almost certainly result in a 'guilty' verdict anyway: he may as well admit it and get some credit for not wasting court time.

It was a very different Bell that faced Webb and Newton when they interviewed him for the second time. He was white-faced, teary-eyed and looking downwards. His solicitor prompted him a few times. Bell admitted that he had killed Crosby but tried to make some excuses for himself: he was in a poor mental state since his wife had just left him, he was trying to save Burwell's family as well as himself, and that he meant merely to confront Crosby, but it got out of hand.

"So you waited half an hour in the bushes with a bit of pipe in your hand just to have a polite word? Don't make me laugh!" snorted Webb in derision. "Why couldn't you have called him into the office at work? What had he done to make you so upset then? Is this what you mean by confronting Crosby? A coward's attack from behind?" Webb drew some graphic photographs from the envelope in front of him and threw them onto the table. They were close-ups of the head injuries taken by forensics. Bell turned away at first, fearing what he would see. "Go on, look at them!" seethed Webb. "For the evidence recording, I am showing Mr Bell two photographs of the head injuries suffered by Mr Crosby." Curiosity overtook Bell, who took a quick glance at the stomach-turning mess before looking away again quickly. Anguish appeared on his face.

"So, why did you do all that?" prompted Webb. After a pause, Bell falteringly tried to give an explanation.

"On Saturday, Graham was outside the back door breaking up cartons and putting them into the recycling bin. Carl was on the cash desk, and I was in my office. One of the carwash lads had come over to use the toilet we have out there. I overheard Graham speak to him in Polish or whatever language it was. I have no idea what was said. I didn't know he could do that and was afraid that he might cause trouble. Their boss doesn't like them mixing with anyone. When Graham came inside, he went on the till to relieve Carl for lunch. I went back to my office to try to decide what to do. It was no use phoning Colin Burwell: he panics at the best of times. I couldn't decide whether Graham had just been saying 'hello' innocently or something more.

Just then, I looked at the CCTV monitor. The shop was empty, and he was diving down behind the till, where the foreign fags were stored. I went in and surprised him and asked him what the hell he thought he was doing. He said that he had dropped a one pound coin from a customer and was trying to retrieve it to put into the till. Another time I might have believed him, but with what had just happened, I guessed that he had found out what was happening.

Carl returned from lunch and was still there the rest of the day, so that I couldn't do anything then. I was relieving duty over at the other garage on Sunday. On Monday, I overheard him say to Carl that he was going to the pub to watch the rugby on Sky TV. I checked in the paper, and it finished at 7:30 pm. I knew where he lived, on Talbot Road, so I guessed he would take the short cut across the Recreation Ground. I waited for him and … (breaks down in sobs). He shouldn't have poked his nose in! I couldn't afford for it to stop: it wasn't just the money. The guys supplying don't take no for an answer once they've drawn you in! At least one of them has a gun."

After pumping Bell for as much information as possible about the Dyzinski brothers and the tobacco suppliers, the pair of detectives switched off the tape and went back to the office. "Jobs a good 'un", announced Webb to the team. Now don't disturb DS Newton: he has a long and very interesting confession to transcribe from the tape. I am going to ring Crown Prosecution

Service with the good news, followed by His Lordship."

"You may like to add another bit of information to it, sir," said DC Catchpole. "Burwell tried to say that transfers from his business to another account were to repay a private loan. Between us, we have already proved this morning for it to be a bogus offshore account set up with fraudulent documents but using his photo. It looks like he was laundering the proceeds of his crimes through it, so we have got the account frozen. It will be that, a motor cruiser that DC Gatesby located at Ipswich Marina plus any watches, jewellery, the house or cash that can be seized here in the UK."

"Brilliant! Money laundering as well! Get the specialist forensic accountant chap to examine it. He is specially trained to spot other stuff that you may not have found and has a lot more time to do it. Well done, all of you, for what you have unearthed already – hit them where it hurts, eh? I wonder if he has been doing it for any other ne'er do wells?" Chuckling, he went into his office and straight for the bag of humbugs. They didn't calm him down how cigarettes used to, but there was the childish pleasure of crunching them into a minty overload in his mouth.

Chapter 13. Wednesday, 2nd December, Ipswich.

Never had the dog walkers seen each other so neatly dressed before. Their dogs, too, had been bathed and brushed to magnificence, whether they appreciated it or not. They sat together with partners in a line of seats in the grandiose Ipswich Town Hall. Gilly had brought her dog Millie, the handsome Dalmation, rather than any of her client's canines. Norma sat between her husband and Sandra, holding onto Bella. Sandra (praying that Jimbo would not start barking) and Norma nudged each other when Jim (with Rex) and Gilly had entered together. Veronica rather self-consciously entered with her partner Carol and the spaniels, but nobody was surprised. John had left his wife at home with a carer and struggled to make Fi sit still. Of course, Stan and Louise were there together with James, who lay on the polished floor sleeping.

The Mayor and The Chief Constable entered, accompanied by DCI Webb and DS Newton reluctantly representing their department. The Mayor made a short introduction, and then the Chief Constable had the floor.

"Good afternoon, and thank you all for coming. We policeman are always very grateful for the support and help that most law-abiding members of the public give us. However, it is my delightful duty this afternoon to recognise an extraordinary group of people from Dinbourne.

As you will have read no doubt from the reports from our gentlemen of the press (he nodded and smiled to the reporter and photographer in attendance), they made extraordinary efforts in helping us to catch major criminals. The men were allegedly involved in murder, tax fraud, modern slavery, money laundering and many other grave crimes. Therefore, I am delighted to present each of our valued citizens of the Dinbourne community with a commendation certificate and a bag of doggy treats for each of their companions! Congratulations to all the Dog Walk Detectives!

Each was called up by their name and dogs name to have handshakes with the Chief Constable and Mayor, a few congratulatory words to owners and dogs, plus the certificate and treats handed to them. The rest of the assembly applauded enthusiastically. Afterwards, the press took endless photographs due to dogs repeatedly facing the wrong way. They appeared on the Suffolk Argus's front page two days later with the headline 'Crime-fighting dog walk detectives receive awards."

The Dog Walk Detectives all returned home to Dinbourne proudly. On the way back, James the Labrador was lying across the car's back seat with Louise and Stan in the front. He somehow managed to break into the bag of biscuits on the car floor and quietly eat them all before he was noticed.

About the author

Pete Jennings was born in Ipswich, Suffolk, in 1953. He has had careers as a telephone engineer, sales manager and recently retired as a registered social worker. He is also a registered psychotherapist and now lives on the Essex / Suffolk border. Some people are held up as shining examples to others; Pete prefers to be an ominous warning.

Outside of his inner working life, Pete has sung with rock and folk bands, been a disco deejay and radio presenter, Anglo Saxon & Viking re-enactor, actor, folklorist, artist, ghost tour guide, storyteller & Pagan activist. He has had over twenty-five books published and regularly lectures in the UK and abroad.

He has a low boredom threshold, likes dogs, 70s prog rock, books, folk traditions, weird humour, real ale and wife Sue, but not necessarily in that order. One day he hopes to be recognised for his pioneering research on the Speed of Dark.

Pete regularly writes shorter magazine articles and reviews, especially for *Widowinde*, *Witchcraft & Wicca, Pagan Dawn* and *Pentacle*. He was also the editor of the *Gippeswic* magazine.

For the full expose of what he gets up to with incriminating photos see www.gippeswic.org

You can also follow Pete Jennings & *Ealdfaeder Anglo Saxons* on Facebook.

For appearances of Pete with his *Ealdfaeder Anglo Saxons* re-enactor friends, plus lots of information on Anglo Saxon topics, go to www.ealdfaeder.org

Other Books & eBooks by Pete Jennings

Pathworking (with Pete Sawyer) – Capall Bann (1993)
Northern Tradition Information Pack – Pagan Federation (1996)
Supernatural Ipswich – Gruff (1997)
Pagan Paths – Rider (2002)
The Northern Tradition – Capall Bann (2003)
Mysterious Ipswich – Gruff (2003)
Old Glory & the Cutty Wren – Gruff (2003)
Pagan Humour – Gruff (2005)
The Gothi & the Rune Stave – Gruff (2005)
Haunted Suffolk – Tempus (2006)
Tales & Tours – Gruff (2006)
Haunted Ipswich – Tempus/ History Press (2010)
Penda: Heathen King of Mercia and his Anglo-Saxon World. – Gruff (2013)
The Wild Hunt & its followers – Gruff (2013)
Blacksmith Gods, Myths, Magicians & Folklore – Moon Books- Pagan Portals (2014)
Heathen Information Pack (with others) – Pagan Federation (2014)
Confidently Confused – Gruff (2014)
Adventures in Ælphame – Gruff (2015)
Valkyries, selectors of heroes: their roles within Viking & Anglo-Saxon heathen beliefs. - Gruff (2016)
A Cacophony of Corvids: the mythology, facts, behaviour and folklore of ravens, crows, magpies and their relatives. - Gruff (2017)
Heathen Paths (2nd expanded & revised edition): Viking and Anglo-Saxon Pagan Beliefs – Gruff (2018)
The Bounds of Ælphame – Gruff (2019)
The Woodwose in Suffolk & beyond. – Gruff (2019)
Pathworking & Creative Visualisation – Gruff (2019)
Viking Warrior Cults – Gruff (2019)
When the sea turned to beer – Gruff (2020)
The Wyrd of Aelphame – Gruff (2020)

Pete Jennings has also contributed to:
Modern Pagans: an investigation of contemporary Pagan practices. (Eds. V Vale & J. Sulak.) San Francisco, USA: RE/Search (2001)
The Museum of Witchcraft: A Magical History – (Ed. Kerriann Godwin) Boscastle: Occult Art Co. (2011)
Heathen Information Pack – UK: Pagan Federation (2014)
The Call of the God: an anthology exploring the divine masculine within modern Paganism (Ed. Frances Billinghurst) Australia: TDM (2015)
Pagan Planet: Being, Believing & Belonging in the 21st Century. Ed. Nimue Brown. UK: Moon Books (2016)

Recordings
Awake (with WYSIWYG) – Homebrew (1987)
Chocks Away (with WYSIWYG) Athos (1988)
No Kidding (with Pyramid of Goats) – Gruff (1990)
Spooky Suffolk (with Ed Nicholls) Gruff (2003)
Old Glory & the Cutty Wren CD – Gruff (2003)

Films that Pete has featured in
Suffolk Ghosts – Directed by Richard Felix. Past in Pictures, 2005
Wild Hunt – Directed by Will Wright. Film Tribe, 2006
In search of Beowulf with Michael Wood BBC4, 2009
Born of Hope – Directed by Kate Maddison – Actors at Work 2009
The Last Journey – Directed by Carl Stickley, 2018

Find details of how to obtain these books and an up to date diary of lectures and appearances by Pete Jennings at www.gippeswic.org
Most books are available as hard copy and electronic digital versions via
www.amazon.co.uk/Pete-Jennings/e/B0034OPQP8

Printed in Great Britain
by Amazon